Guarding Amber

The Waystation Guardians
Book 2

By
KateMarie Collins

ALL RIGHTS RESERVED

Publisher's Note:

This is a work of fiction. All names, characters, places, and events are the work of the author's imagination.

Any resemblance to real persons, places, or events is coincidental.

Solstice Publishing - www.solsticepublishing.com

For Mo

Nothing but the rain

Chapter One
Full Moon

Amber bolted the door for the night and walked into the living room. Stuffing the pouch back into its hiding place within the brick fireplace, she felt Minerva rub against her legs.

"Yeah, I know. Tonight was a hard one," she said, her voice tired. Reaching down to pick up the calico cat, she nuzzled her face into Minerva's furry body. "Come on," she said as she started toward the staircase. "I need some sleep."

The cat leaped from her arms as they reached the top of the stairs. The light of her computer screen caught her notice. *Damn*, she thought, *I need to email Kate and let her know I'll be late tomorrow.* She turned and headed into the library. Pulling out the chair in front of her desk, she dashed off a quick email.

At least she'll understand. It's not like I flake on her after every full moon. Kate was fully aware there was something special about the River House. She knew about Charon. What she didn't know was how, some months, the souls that Amber guided onto his boat were anything but peaceful.

She sent the email, and quickly scanned over what was in her inbox. Two notifications about shipped items she'd ordered and some spam thing. *Do people really fall for this crap?* she thought as she sent that one to her junk folder. Her rule of thumb was to delete anything from an address she didn't recognize. That the subject said "URGENT WARNING" in all caps was another red flag.

Setting her computer to do a reboot, she turned off the monitor and rose. She scratched at one side of her head, stretched, and walked through the door that led to her bathroom and then the bedroom. Within five minutes, her phone was plugged into the charger and she was snuggling under the blankets with Minerva curling up beside her.

***

The buzzing kept going off, no matter what Amber did to ignore it. At first, she thought it was part of her dream. It would stop, only to start again a few minutes later. The thought began to creep into her mind that it was her phone. She blindly reached for the side table, her fingers fumbling to pull the charger cord out of the bottom before picking it up.

Opening her eyes, she recognized the number. Larry Dixon, the lawyer who'd worked with her and the inheritance that brought her here from Texas. To her new life.

"Hello?" she answered, closing her eyes again as she plopped back onto her pillows.

"Amber? Thank God! Where are you?" His voice, a mix of relief and fear, jolted the last vestiges of sleep from her body.

"I'm at home, in bed. Why? What's happened?"

"You didn't go in to work with Kate at The Cauldron this morning, then?" She heard him pause and exhale. "Good."

Sitting up, she stared at the foot of her bed. A ball of fear began to form in her stomach. Something was beyond wrong. "Larry, what happened?"

He paused, "Someone left a bomb for you or Kate to find."

"WHAT?!?!?" Amber screamed. "Is Kate okay?"

"She's at the hospital. Jessa told me you were supposed to have a shift this morning before she went to see Kate in the ambulance. Hold on. Let me tell the fire chief that you're fine."

She put the phone on speaker and left it on the bed. Jumping up, she pulled open drawers and grabbed for clothes. Not caring what she wore. Finding out that Kate was okay, and who bombed the store, was more important than anything else.

"Amber?" Larry's voice called out from the bed.

"I've got you on speaker. I'll head to the hospital in a few."

"Okay. I'll meet you there. There's nothing I can do here anyway."

Amber picked the phone up as she shoved her feet into a pair of flats at the edge of the bed. "Larry? Was anyone else hurt?"

"Not that I know of."

"What about the shop?"

"The damage was contained to just The Cauldron. The rest of the block's okay. It's pretty extensive, though."

Her heart sank even further. The Cauldron was Kate's baby. She put her heart and soul into her shop, both the brick and mortar version and the online one. It would hurt her to know it was gone as much as the physical damage to her body. "See you there," she said as she disconnected the call. Shoving her phone into the pocket of her jeans, she ran down the stairs. Grabbing her purse and keys, she stopped long enough to lock the door behind her.

"Please be okay," she muttered under her breath as she anxiously waited for the garage door to raise so she could get her SUV moving.

It took every ounce of her self-control not to speed on the way to the hospital. Kate was her best friend in Cavendish, had been a friend of her great-aunt. Even helped her explore Wicca without being judgmental or pushy. She was not ready to guide her onto Charon's boat.

Her tires squealed as she took the corner into the hospital's parking lot too fast. *Slow down,* she screamed in her mind. *You're not going to help Kate if you're in the hospital, too!*

She pulled into an empty space and jammed the car into park. One hand reached to undo her seatbelt as the other twisted the key so hard she thought she'd broken it for a moment. Her hands shook. Closing her eyes, Amber took a few deep, calming breaths. Nothing would change if she ran in there in a panic. If Kate was going to be okay, it was up to the doctors and nurses. And Kate's own will to recover.

Once she found her center and calmed down, she slung her bag over her head. Putting her cell on vibrate, she shoved it in the front pocket of her jeans along with her keys. She glanced around for traffic before striding to the big sliding doors under the EMERGENCY sign.

The room was quiet. Too quiet. A nurse stood behind a long counter, shuffling metal clipboards.

"Excuse me," Amber said as she approached the desk. "I need to know what happened to my friend, Kate Warfield-Duff."

"Are you a relative?" The nurse barely glanced at her before returning to her sorting.

Amber blinked, "Well, no. She's my best friend, and my boss."

"Privacy laws prohibit releasing any information without the patient's consent. Now," she thrust out her chin toward the small array of chairs, "if you'd like to have a seat and wait until family shows up, you can." She turned her back to Amber and started to go through more charts.

Sighing, Amber ran her hand through her hair. Not knowing what else to do, she wandered over to the waiting area.

Pulling the phone out of her pocket, she unlocked it and pulled up Heath's number. No, she decided. He'd still be at the scene. If what Larry had said on the phone was accurate, the entire fire department was on the scene. Including the volunteers, like Heath.

She didn't have Jessa's number, either. Then again, she was probably in another waiting room in the hospital. Neither Kate nor Jessa felt the overwhelming need to be married to cement their partnership. But, when it was legal to do so, they thought it was best. Jessa was Kate's spouse. No nurse would be able to keep her from learning what was going on.

The doors moved, the muggy late summer air coming in behind Larry and Jessa. Amber rose, heading their way.

Jessa made a beeline for the desk. Hanging back, Amber looked at Larry. "What happened?"

He motioned for them to move back into the waiting area. "All Jessa's said is that she and Kate were running late this morning. She dropped her off at the front of the store and saw her bend down to pick up a box that sat at the entry. She was heading to her office when she saw the explosion in her rear-view mirror."

"She's in surgery," Jessa's voice came from behind Amber. "The nurse said we can head up to the second floor and wait. If I'm lucky, there'll be a nurse up there who can ask what's going on. Otherwise, we wait for the surgeon to come out."

"I'll wait with you if you want me to."

Jessa smiled slightly, "That would be good. I'm not calling her parents yet. Not until we know what the prognosis is. No reason for them to come out when we really don't know much."

Larry cleared his throat, "Jessa, you have Amber give me a call if you need me for anything. I'm going to go back, see if Officer Taylor has any leads. Make sure the shop can be secured so no one tries to steal anything."

Amber turned to him, "Larry, once I know how Kate is, I'd like to go down there. The Cauldron's her baby.

If I can get started on the clean-up, keep the online store open, it'll take one worry off of her."

The older man nodded. "Give me a call when you want to head over. I'll clear it with the authorities. If that's okay with you, Jessa?"

"Yeah, that's fine. I'm heading upstairs. I need to know what's going on with Kate." She started walking toward an elevator.

"I'll call you later, Larry," Amber called out as she moved to catch up.

They rode in silence in the elevator. Amber wasn't sure what to say to Jessa. While she and Kate worked closely with each other in the shop, Amber hadn't spent enough time around Jessa to know the words to use. They were both worried about the same person, that was a given.

The car jolted to a stop, and the doors opened on one end. Following Jessa out, Amber hung back in the waiting area. Generic plastic plants, a tank with fish, and a variety of chairs dotted the space. Amber glanced up at the televisions mounted on the wall. One showed some vapid game show. *They still have those on?* Amber thought, amazed. Her mom used to watch game shows for hours, always certain she knew more than the contestants.

The other monitor showed one set of three numbers, highlighted in yellow. The rest of the screen was blue.

"That's her," Jessa said. Turning, Amber saw her pointing at the screen. "She's in surgery. When it goes to pink, she's in recovery. Outside of that, we won't know anything until the surgeon comes out."

"Did the nurse tell you anything else? Like why she's in surgery?"

Jessa shrugged and moved to one of the chairs. She dropped into it and ran one hand through her blonde hair. "Not really. Only that Kate had multiple lacerations from the blast, possibly some burns." She released a heavy sigh.

Amber sat in a chair next to her. "Well, I'm here. If you need something to eat or anything, just let me know and I'll take care of it."

"Thanks. Right now, I'm not sure what I need. Besides Kate to come out of this."

Amber leaned back and pulled her phone out of her pocket. She pulled up Health's number and sent him a text. "At hospital with Jessa. Waiting on news about Kate."

The screen flashed at her. "BRT."

A few minutes later, the chime of the elevator made Amber raise her head. The door opened, and Heath walked out. Rising, she went to give him a hug. He still wore his turnout pants, the jacket slung over one shoulder.

She melted into his arms, trying not to inhale the smoky scent that lingered on him. Instead, she let herself calm down as his arms surrounded her. "Any word on Kate yet?" Heath's voice was low.

She pulled away and glanced at the monitor. The color hadn't changed. "Nothing yet." She went to grab his hand and saw the plastic bracelet that circled his wrist. "Heath, why'd they admit you to the hospital?"

He raised his arm and tugged at the band as he replied, "Precautionary. Made most of us get checked out. There was something funky in the air and it got into Marc's respirator. Made him lose his breakfast. Captain made us all come in and get checked out." The band finally snapped free. "I'm fine." He looked past her, "Hey, Jessa. You holding up okay?"

Turning her head, Amber saw her approach. "Yeah, I think so." She took a deep breath. "Amber, I know you want to make sure Kate's okay. And I promise to tell you when I know anything. But I need some downtime. I want to be able to ask the surgeon questions. Go look at the shop if they'll let you in. And then head home. I promise to come by once I know she's stable. And she'll recover faster if I can tell her you're spearheading the effort to reopen The Cauldron."

Amber swallowed, trying to keep her disappointment from showing. "Okay, Jessa. If that's what you need me to do."

Jessa reached out and took Amber's hand. "It is. Whatever's going to happen, you staying here and jumping at every bell isn't going to help the outcome.

Nodding, Amber released Jessa's hand after giving it a reassuring squeeze. "Okay. I'll go see how bad the shop is and then head home. Call me when you know something, okay?"

"I will. I promise."

Amber turned and pressed the button for the elevator. She glanced at the monitor one more time.

Kate was still in surgery.

Chapter Two

Once they were in the elevator, Amber pulled out her phone and sent Larry a text to alert him she was heading to the shop. "How bad is it, Heath?" she asked, her voice quiet.

"It's not beyond salvaging. The blast was contained to the first room. The library area and stockroom weren't damaged. There wasn't even any fire to contend with. Just the dust and broken glass from the package, really. The blast sent that crap everywhere." He paused, "I didn't want to say this in front of Jessa, but whoever did this meant to hurt Kate. Or you."

Amber refused to think about that possibility. "Any idea what was in the dust?"

Heath shook his head. "Not yet, but they took samples from our gear. Nurse went fishing for a vein on me to get blood, too. I'm sure they'll figure it out after a few days."

The elevator stopped on the main floor, the doors opening to a full waiting room. Amber waited as Heath greeted a few friends who were still getting cleared after working the scene.

Her phone buzzed. A text from Larry flashed on her screen, "Meet you there."

She placed a hand on Heath's back, getting his attention. "Larry's waiting for me. You got a ride home?"

"Uh, yeah…I'll catch a ride with one of the guys. I'll swing by your place once I get cleaned up."

She gave him a quick kiss and headed out the doors.

Knowing she'd keep watching for the text from Jessa, Amber placed her phone inside the center console box of her SUV. It was a short drive to downtown, where The Cauldron was. The street was still blocked off by police cars and one fire engine. Weaving her way around onlookers and traffic, she found a parking spot.

Digging her phone out, she sighed at the screen. No messages. Grabbing her purse, she got out and locked the vehicle before shoving the keys in her pocket.

Most of the crowd had left. Nothing left to gawk at. She dodged a few people as she made for the closest police officer. Rather than looking at The Cauldron, she kept an eye out for Larry.

"Stay back, miss."

Amber stopped at the barrier and looked at the officer. "My name's Amber Cross. I work with Kate at The Cauldron. Larry Dixon wanted me to come here and help assess the damage."

The cop held up his hand. "I gotta check before I can let you in there." He pushed the side of the handset attached to the shoulder of his uniform. "Chief? Got someone up here who's looking for Larry. Says she works in the store."

A muffled reply came across, and the officer spoke again. "Roger that." He turned his attention back to her. "Larry's on his way up here. If he vouches for you, then you can come into the area. But not until then."

Nodding, she sighed. No use arguing with him.

"Oh, hey Amber." A voice called out behind her.

Turning, she saw Heidi coming closer to the barricade, a tray with four cups in it balanced in her hands. "Hi," she replied as she stepped aside. She waited for Heidi to finish handing the drinks over to the officer. They weren't close, by any stretch of the imagination. Amber wasn't sure how, but the other woman had changed after the news came about her husband. One final tour and he was going to retire. Then a roadside bomb took out the transport he was riding in. Heidi hadn't been the same person ever since the news came. She still ran her café and kept up appearances. But something in her died when he did.

"It's sad, isn't it?" Heidi's voice broke through Amber's thoughts. "I'll miss Kate and Jessa."

Blinking in confusion, Amber asked, "Miss them? I don't know what you mean."

Heidi shrugged, her blonde ponytail bobbing slightly. "Well, with the business gone, I can't imagine staying here. Jessa can always find another job in marketing. She used to work at a big firm in Bangor. That's where she and Kate met. When our dad got sick…that's when they moved back here. He's gone…the shop's gone…not much reason for them to stay now." Her gaze turned back down the street toward the shop.

"Maybe they like it here. Or have friends."

"It's possible, but I think they'll move. Once Kate can, that is." She looked back at Amber. "I'm not sure why Heath stopped coming, but you really should both come to church. People might think you're as crazy as your great-aunt was."

Amber drew a deep breath, forcing herself to calm down. "Heidi, my great-aunt wasn't crazy. And I don't keep Heath from going. If that's what he wants to do."

"Of course you don't," she smirked. But the smile didn't reach her eyes. "I need to get back to the shop before the oldest starts giving away food. I'll swing by the hospital and bring Jessa some dinner later on."

Before she could reply, Heidi turned and walked away from Amber. She watched, puzzled. She knew Heidi and Jessa were sisters, but that's where any similarities ended.

"Amber."

Turning, she saw Larry standing next to the officer. "She's okay," he said as he waived her inside the cordoned off area.

"How's Kate?"

"Don't know yet. Jessa hasn't texted me, so she might still be in surgery."

Larry nodded, "The hospital's a good one. And you can have a quiet life here, too. I'm sure she's in good hands." He guided Amber around the emergency vehicles. "The front window's gone, and they've got that boarded up now. They'll have to do the same to the door to keep people out."

A couple of firefighters were pulling off hazmat suits and nodded at her as she went past them. They were friends of Heath's, but she couldn't remember their names.

"I've got a key to the back. So does Jessa."

"Good. What we need now is a quick look, let us know if there's anything you see right off that's missing. The team's already cleared it for any potential airborne issues, but wear these to be safe." He handed her a pair of rubber gloves and a face mask. "Tomorrow, when you know Kate's going to be okay, you can come in and start doing a real inventory of the damage. They're going to keep some fans running tonight, to clear out whatever the dust was in the package."

She stopped as they came up alongside the store. Her heart sank. The sidewalk was littered with glass and bits of wood. The picture window to the right of the door was completely gone. The brick wall on the left, where the library was, showed a few cracks but no additional damage.

Reaching into her pocket, she pulled out her phone. "I want to take pictures to show Jessa and Kate," she told him as she finished putting on the safety gear.

Larry nodded. "Be careful."

She moved carefully, avoiding both large shards of glass and the last of the crew working to clean up. Stepping across the threshold, she took a good look at the damage.

The scent of sage almost overwhelmed her. Heath was right. There wasn't much actual damage. The case holding crystal orbs and geodes was shattered, the contents either off their stands or scattered on the floor. The center table was covered with a dark brown dust that coated the myriad of pendulums and pendants. A green wallet, Kate's, rested on it, next to her keys. *She must've put things there to see what was in the package,* Amber thought. She stepped around the broken mosaic tiles on the floor from the mural that had decorated the wall. The colors always made her smile. It would take months to re-create.

She walked around the wall and into the classroom. Books littered the floor, shaken loose from the blast. Moving purposefully, she strode over and started to pick them up. *I'll shelve them tomorrow,* she thought, *but at least they'll be off the floor.*

The storeroom was fine. Just to be thorough, Amber did a quick visual on the safe. Nothing on it made her think anyone had tried to get into it. She slid into the chair in front of the computer they'd used to maintain the website. Logging in, she made a quick post that there'd been a personal issue but that orders would only be delayed by a day or two. *I have to keep things going. Give Kate one less thing to worry about as she recovers.* Checking the email, she knew not to delete anything. Everything would stay there unless an order was filled and shipped, or Kate deleted it. Even the spam mail.

Her throat began to dry out. Remembering how Heath and his friends had gone to the hospital as a precaution, she logged off the computer quickly and turned it off. The sage smell was still strong, even back here. Curious, she pulled a small empty amber vial from one of the containers. It wouldn't hold much, but it would be enough to work with.

Working her way back out to the main entry, she stopped by Kate's wallet and keys. She unscrewed the lid of the bottle and, using a business card from the pile strewn across the table, funneled some of the powder into the container. She screwed the lid tight and shoved it into her pocket. Reaching out for the other two items, she stopped. The dust was all over them. She darted behind the register area, swearing under her breath. There wasn't any dust back there. Reaching down, she grabbed a paper bag off the top of the stack. Pulling open a drawer, she pulled out a couple of pieces of tissue paper. Walking back to the table, she used the tissue to pick up the items and put them in the bag before walking out.

"I'll be able to get things running pretty easily," she said as she came up to Larry. "The mosaic's damaged, and some of the crystals and orbs may be cracked. The case was shattered. I'd like to keep these," she held up the paper bag, "to give over to Jessa. She promised to come by later tonight."

"You be careful with that dust." Larry advised her.

"I will be. I'll keep Minerva away from it, too." She sighed, "I'll be back tomorrow, make sure the online orders get filled as much as possible. I won't open it back up until Kate's ready to do that, though." She paused, "Larry, was there anything they've found yet to say who did this? Or why?"

He held his arm out, motioning her to move back away from the shop. "No, not that I know of," he said as they walked down the street. The fire engines were gone now. A recovery crew had pulled up and started to unload some industrial fans. "I can't think of anyone that might want to hurt her, either. Can you?

Amber shook her head. "No. And that's what bothers me."

Larry put his hand on her arm, and she stopped. "Amber, we have to think about it in relation to you as much as we do Kate. It's not like you had people who really accepted how you left Louden. It's possible this was aimed at you, not her."

Amber fought against the fear rising within her. "But…Bruce…he's dead. They said it was a bear…" she whispered.

"I know. But you told me yourself. He had a large circle of friends. Most of whom thought like he did." He took her by the elbow and started them moving again. "I just want you to think about the possibilities, Amber. Watch your back, don't take chances. Until this is sorted out and the sheriff's done with his investigation, you have to be cautious." They stepped around the barrier. "Where are you parked?"

"Over there," she pointed, "behind the bank."

They turned and kept walking. "Stay home when you can. Call me when you're coming in here and leaving again. I'll talk to Sheriff Taylor about having someone keep an eye on the store when you're working."

She stopped and looked at him. "Larry, I understand your concern. I really do. And I know you probably promised Amanda to look out for me. But I'm done with living my life in fear. Bruce is dead. No one from Texas has even come close to trying to find me here. They buried Grace. So did I. I'm Amber Cross now. And I'm not going to run scared."

Larry smiled, "Your aunt would've said the same thing. Okay, do what you're going to do. But let me know before you do anything crazy, please?"

Smiling back at him, she said, "Dunno about that. There's a whole lot of things that I do that most people would classify as crazy." Turning away from him, she sauntered over to her car. Once she knew he couldn't see her, she pulled the vial of dust out of her pocket.

"Sorry, Larry," she said as she started the ignition. "But I have to find out what was in that dust and I can't wait for the state crime lab to do it for me."

She waved at him one more time as she pulled out of the parking lot and headed back to the River House.

Chapter Three

Amber sat on a pillow, leaning against the sofa. The coffee table before her had transformed into a workspace. She'd removed all the magazines and remotes when she got home. Dashing around the house, she'd gathered a variety of tools. Everything from incense burners and charcoal to bottled water and closely woven linen. After that, she'd brought down about a dozen books from the library, along with pen and paper.

Then, she got to work.

Sighing, she tossed the pen onto the pad full of notes. She moved her neck slowly to each side, feeling the muscles protest. She was close, and she knew it. But she'd still only been able to isolate two of the ingredients in the dust.

And she was halfway through what she'd scooped up.

Her doorbell rang. Reaching for her phone, she opened the app connected to the security camera. Heath stood at the door, holding a pizza box. Her stomach growled. Punching in the code, she unlocked the door. Then reached for her notes again.

"Amber?" Heath called out.

"I'm in here," she responded.

"Hey," he said. She looked up and saw him half in the doorway to the room. "Want me to grab some plates and stuff?"

She put the pad back on the table and reached for the next book on the pile next to her. "Sure."

Amber began to flip through the pages, hoping there was an index she could cross reference. Sage was a definite factor. And she'd found evidence of lemon verbena as well. But what else? And why combine them into a bomb?

"Amber? Hon?"

She lifted her head, not realizing Heath was talking to her. "Sorry," she muttered as she used a finger to mark her spot in the book. "I wasn't listening. What did you say?"

"I asked if you wanted anything to drink," he replied as he placed the pizza on a side table. Plates and napkins sat on the top of the box.

"Oh, no. Thanks." She pointed to the bottle of water resting on the table. "I'm good."

Heath started to sit on the floor when the doorbell rang out again. Amber looked at her phone. "It's Jessa," she said.

"Stay there," he replied, straightening up. "I'll let her in and then grab another plate."

"Thanks." She tore a corner of paper off the pad and placed it in the book. Setting it back on the floor, she pushed herself up as Jessa came into the room.

"Kate's out of surgery."

Amber let out a long breath, "That's good, right?"

The blonde woman sank into an overstuffed chair with a sigh. "They say so, but I'm not entirely sure. I was only able to see her for a few minutes. She's not waking up. And her skin's covered with small welts. I haven't seen it like that since..." Her voice trailed off and her eyes went wide.

"Since when?"

Jessa leaned forward, her face tightened. "When we went to Scotland and England on our honeymoon. One of the places we stayed at had this amazing rose garden. Varieties I'd never seen. Kate got the same welts on her hands and face when she leaned over to smell one of them. Owner said it was agrimony. We found a doctor and he said it was an allergic reaction, gave her a cream to put on it. It cleared up pretty fast. Kate said she'd have to make sure it wasn't in the shop or that only you handled it if she ever decided to stock it." She fumbled through her purse, searching, "I have to call the hospital." Rising, she strode out of the room.

"What happened?" Heath asked as he entered the room.

"Jessa remembered something about an allergy Kate has…" her focus shifted to the pile of books. She dropped to the floor, shuffling through the tomes until she found the one she was looking for. *Please, no…not that,* she thought as she flipped furiously through the pages. When she came to the page she needed, her heart sank as she read the header for the spell.

To banish a soul and make it leave your presence.

Take leaves of agrimony and crush them on a waning moon.

Add sage, lemon verbena, and hen-

"Doctor said he'd start treating her right away." Jessa's voice interrupted Amber's reading.

Looking up, Amber asked, "Did he say anything else? Did Kate have any other allergies?"

"He said the lab had gotten some preliminary reports on the dust that was on her skin. Why?"

Rising, she held the book out to Jessa. "Were any of the things he said on this list?"

Taking the book, Jessa read over the page. "Yes," she said. "All of them." She looked at Amber. "Are you trying to say a Wiccan's behind this? That they tried to banish her soul?"

Amber ran a hand through her hair. "I don't know. With the Internet, a lot of this information's easy to find. Given how much dust was in the package, who knows what it really did? I doubt it was a Wiccan. We don't harm people, and we certainly don't try to banish souls! We might ask for help in keeping negativity out of our lives, but that's it." She paused, thinking. "The delivery was totally wrong. A Wiccan would've done small quantities in a cauldron, in a Circle cast in their own sacred space. To deliver it via a bomb…it's just not our way. Besides, we don't know if Kate was the target yet, or I was. If you'll let me, I want to see her."

Jessa nodded, "Sure. Tomorrow, though. They sent me home because they put her in ICU for tonight. Want to give her some time to recover from surgery and all that."

Amber took the book back and placed it on the table before sitting down. Suddenly, a plate with a slice of pizza showed up in front of her. Looking up, she smiled at Heath. "Thanks," she said as she started to eat.

Jessa dug into the slice he offered her. "I haven't eaten all day," she muttered.

"I ran into Heidi on my way to The Cauldron. She said she was taking you some food. Didn't she show up?"

Jessa shrugged, "Nope. But that's her way. She tells everyone that she does things for me so she looks like the good sister. In reality, the food's probably in her fridge for her kids to eat. I don't mind. I'm used to how she is."

They ate in silence. Amber's mind refused to be quiet, though. Who would want her or Kate out of town so much that they'd resort to these measures?

"Jessa, I really don't think this was a Wiccan. It doesn't feel right. The store is covered in the dust. The way the spell reads, it's not the right way to distribute the intent. It should've been done in a sacred space, with just the caster present. And something of the target to burn with the herbs. The front part of the store is covered in this dust. Kate would've inhaled it, had it on her skin. But there's nothing in the text that says to do it that way. It's overkill."

Jessa put down her plate. "I really don't know, Amber. Right now, I just want to know that she's going to be okay."

Remembering the items she'd grabbed from the store, she rose. "Hold on. The fire chief let me take some stuff back here from the store." She walked down the hall to the mudroom. Above the row of coat hooks, she pulled down Kate's wallet and keys. She'd stashed them up there after cleaning the dust off of them outside. "I didn't want these left in the store," she said as she walked back in the room and handed them to Jessa.

"Thanks," she said with a smile. She rose from the chair and tucked the wallet and keys into her purse. "I'm heading back to the hospital for a few, then home. I'll let you know if anything changes tonight, and make sure you're on the visitor list. Thanks for the pizza."

Amber walked with her to the front door. "Anytime. You know you can crash here if you don't want to go home tonight."

Jessa nodded and hugged Amber before walking out the door.

Twisting the dead bolt, she watched through the slim panel of stained glass to one side of the door as the other woman strode down the walkway to her car. "You didn't tell her everything." Heath's voice was just behind her.

"No, I didn't." Amber sighed. "I didn't see any reason to worry her."

"Do I get to know? Or are you keeping everyone in the dark?" His tone was sarcastic.

Turning, she looked at him. "What's wrong?" she asked. "You know there's reasons why I had secrets. I've told you everything you need to know. I'm not trying to keep you or anyone in the dark. Jessa doesn't need to know about what happens here, or about Texas." Amber looked at him, confused.

Heath crossed his arms and leaned against the wall. "So, why are you so sure a Wiccan couldn't have done this to Kate? Or that you're not the target and she got in the way? Come on, Amber. Use your head! You were supposed to work this morning. It could be you in that hospital, not Kate! What did that book tell you that you didn't tell Jessa? That you're not telling me?"

She cocked her head to one side, trying not to let anger overtake her at his words. "Excuse me? 'Use my head'? I'm not stupid, Heath. Don't ever think I am. And I'm not going to tell anyone else when I don't have anything beyond suspicions. It's called needing proof! I'm not going to jump to conclusions like Louise did!" Her voice was rising. The idea that he thought she wasn't thinking things through made her blood boil. "All I know at this point is what was in the dust. That's it. What point is there to tell Jessa when I don't know beyond that?"

"Fine. Tell me, then! Or don't you trust me with the secret, either?"

She looked at him. His arms were crossed, and his jaw moved as he clenched the muscles. Most likely, he wouldn't believe her if she told him. Not in the state he was in. "No," she said, her voice calm and even. "I'm not going to tell anyone until I have proof. And I won't have that until I see Kate tomorrow."

He threw his arms up and moved into the living room. "Whatever. You're not in a mood to talk to me. I'll read the damn book myself and figure it out."

"Go home, Heath." She unlocked the front door and opened it.

Heath stopped and turned around. "What are you talking about?"

"Get out of my house. I need to do a lot of reading and research. I can't do that with you here, fighting me."

"I'm not the one who won't talk!"

She gave him a direct look. "Go back to your apartment. I don't want you here tonight."

He stared at her, then moved toward the door. For a moment, he stopped and opened his mouth. She glared at him and he shut it as he stormed outside. Whatever he was going to say, he decided not to.

She closed the door behind him, locking it and arming the security system.

"Meow."

Bending down, she picked up the calico cat. "Come on, Minerva," she said as she stroked her fur. "Let's see if we can find out why someone would want to sever Kate's soul and send it to the Underworld."

"Meow."

Chapter Four

Something furry pushed against her, followed by a wetness. Sighing, Amber raised her hand and scratched at Minerva without opening her eyes. The cat purred in appreciation. She let her mind wake up more before she tried to move. The couch wasn't nearly as comfortable to sleep on as she thought it would've been.

Light filtered through the curtains. "How late is it, Minerva?" she asked.

The cat didn't answer. Instead, it jumped off her chest. Amber rubbed at her eyes and sat up.

She'd cleaned up most of the stuff last night after Heath left. *Correction*, she told herself. *After I threw him out.* She knew what the dust contained, and why they were mixed together. Definitely wasn't another Wiccan that did this. Even someone who was mad about an order wouldn't go to this extreme.

Picking up the pencil, she ran through her notes again. It wasn't a witch, but someone who wanted Kate or her gone. "It's almost clumsy," she muttered. "Like someone who wanted to look like they knew what they were doing. But really didn't."

The pile of books had been re-shelved. She'd only kept out the one with the spell she'd found in it. None of the others had the same combination of herbs.

She flipped to the marked page again. What had happened wasn't the intent. Like most banishing spells, it was meant to simply make the person go away. Find another individual to mess with. Outside of the agrimony, which Kate was allergic to, nothing was harmful if cast the way the spell was intended.

But something had gone off the rails. The delivery, the amount of powder used. It shouldn't have made anyone sick. Something else was going on.

Her phone chimed, warning her that the battery was low. She swiped it off the table as she headed to the kitchen. One text from Jessa. "She's still in a coma, they're giving her an MRI at nine. Should be back in her room by ten, but you can't stay long. They're trying to keep her isolated because of the allergy. Room 305."

She glanced at the time on the microwave as she entered the kitchen. 8:30. Good. She had time to shower before she headed over. She connected the phone to a charger and fed Minerva.

It buzzed again. This time, Heath's name popped up on the screen. *I'm not ready for that conversation yet*, she thought. Turning her back on the phone, she sprinted upstairs.

Once out of the shower, she sat down at the computer desk for a minute. She went to her email, intent to check on the packages coming in. There was the scammer again. Sighing, she moved it over to her junk folder and then deleted it. "Urgent warning, my ass," she muttered. "All you want is money." Rising, she got up to return the towel to its spot in the bathroom and get dressed and go.

She pulled the SUV up alongside her favorite coffee stand. "Hey, Joyce! Can I get a tall Irish cream breve latte, hot?"

"Sure, Amber." The blonde barista moved away from the window and over to the espresso machine. "I'm sorry to hear about Kate," she said as she worked on Amber's drink. "Any word on her condition yet?"

"Not really. Jessa sent me a text today, said they were running another test this morning. I'm heading over there to check in with her before I go into the shop."

"Well, let her know we're thinking of her," Joyce slipped the cup into a sleeve and poked two straws through the lid before handing it over to Amber. "That's $3.86."

Pulling a five-dollar bill out of her wallet, she handed it over and said, "Rest is yours."

"Thanks!" She opened the till, then looked back at Amber. "You think the shop will open back up, then?"

Nodding, she replied. "I do. There really isn't a lot of damage to the merchandise. I'm going to keep the online orders going out as much as I can while she recovers."

"Good. I was thinking of taking the meditation class Kate was talking about starting up. I understand it might not start on schedule, but I'm interested! Would you let me know when she's ready to start sign ups?"

Amber took a sip of the coffee and savored the taste. "Absolutely!" She held up the cup, "Thanks again!" Putting the cup into a holder, she drove toward the hospital.

Pulling into a parking spot, she drained the last of the coffee as she turned off the engine. Slinging her purse across her body, she got out and walked into the hospital.

She checked the time on her phone. It was just after ten. Heath had sent her another text, but she didn't read it. *Not until I know how Kate's doing*, she told herself. *I can only deal with one crisis at a time.* Once in the elevator, she made sure the phone was still on silent.

Stepping off the elevator, she followed the arrows toward Kate's room. Jessa stood outside, in the hallway.

"Jessa, how is she?"

"The same. They're getting her back in the room now."

"What'd the scan show?"

"Nothing. That's the problem. They can't find a reason why she's in the coma. The damage to her wasn't that bad. The bleeding they got under control in the OR yesterday. Set a broken bone in her wrist at the same time. That doesn't explain the coma. It's not her allergy, either."

Two nurses started to wheel a bed out of the room. Amber and Jessa moved aside, giving them room.

She stood back, waiting for Jessa to go in first. Taking a moment, she found her center and then crossed the threshold.

Kate lay on the bed, her face and arms covered with some sort of cream. The gentle rise and fall of the blanket, along with the steady beep of monitors, were the only indication that she was alive. A single I.V. snaked from her left arm into a bag hanging from a pole. The clear liquid dripping at a slow, measured pace. Another needle rested in her right arm, the tubing looping across her palm but it wasn't connected to anything. "I've asked them several times to take that one out," Jessa mentioned, nodding at Kate's right side. "Kate's so right-handed, that one's going to drive her nuts when she wakes up. They say they won't, though. Something about having it there in case anything goes wrong." She pushed the button on a small CD player. "I don't know if it helps. I've heard music can. She's always said Chris DeBurgh was her favorite artist that not nearly enough people listened to."

The opening notes of "Don't Pay the Ferryman" began to drift softly from the stereo. Amber smiled. *I wonder if Charon's ever heard about this song?* She thought.

"Do you mind if I stay here?" Jessa asked. "I don't know what you're looking for or anything. Wicca's always been her thing. But I respect the faith."

Amber smiled. "No, you can stay here. It's not that kind of thing. It's more…how do I put it…of me extending my energy to try to find where her soul is."

"Well, whatever you're doing must be working. That pentacle of yours is glowing."

Startled, Amber lifted her hand and placed it around the pendant. It was her great-aunt's, and the one thing she knew she'd always keep. It felt warm, welcoming.

Taking a deep breath, she reached out for Kate's hand with her free one. Closing her eyes, she went searching for her friend.

She found part of Kate's essence, hiding in her mind. It was scared, fragmented. Nightmarish images swirled around her. She saw the explosion that forced the rest of her soul from her body, shredding it in the blast. A single image began to coalesce. A series of concentric rings of land, each one surrounded by a single river. At the outermost ring, a gate. A man, dressed in black, stood as others streamed past him off of a boat. He nodded once to the man at the rudder. The hood fell back from his face.

It was Charon.

With a start, her eyes flew open.

"Amber?" Jessa asked.

Frantically, she tried to come up with something to say. Something that wouldn't scare Jessa. "It's going to be okay. I know it will." She darted around the bed and waved at Jessa. "I've got to go to the store for a few. Make sure the shipments are ready to go."

Jessa's hand reached out and circled her arm, stopping her. "Amber, what is it? What did you learn?"

Her own panic starting to fade, she reached out and held Jessa's hand in both of hers. "I know where Kate's soul went. And I promise I'll find a way to make it return. Stay here, keep talking to her and playing the music. It'll help her find her way."

She let go and dashed out of the room before the other woman could stop her again. Her mind refused to work. *Not in the hospital. Wait until I get in the car. Then I can fall apart.*

Bypassing the elevator, she charged down the stairs. Her heart racing in time with her feet. Reaching the first floor, she all but ran out the main entrance and to her car. Fear was rising fast in her. One that threatened to encompass her.

The key ring jangled as she pushed the unlock button on her key fob. She threw open the door, climbed in, and slammed it shut. Her fingers locked around the steering wheel as she let the sobs finally come.

Kate's soul had been sent to the Underworld, and she didn't have a clue how to find it, let alone bring it back.

She rode the waves of panic and fear, knowing each one was smaller than the last. She hadn't had a panic attack like this for almost a year. Only when the one letter showed up, addressed to Grace Adams. Even dead, Bruce had his claws in her.

It took a few minutes, but she regained control of her breathing. Swiping at the tears on her face, she took some deep breaths. "Focus, damn it," she said. "Go to the store. Do the online orders. Shippers don't come for pick up until after three. Get those out, keep her business running. Tonight, do the research. Find out if it's even possible. One step at a time."

She started the car and headed to The Cauldron.

***

Starting with the pile they'd pulled to fill two days earlier, Amber got to work. Luckily, all the orders were for herbs and tinctures they normally stocked in the back. She wouldn't have to mix anything. The delivery service wouldn't be there until later in the day, which gave her plenty of time. She flipped a few switches on the stereo and cranked up the volume.

Once she got the older orders processed and packaged up, she went out to the damaged area. Rummaging through the cabinets behind the register, she found the box of paper face masks and latex gloves Kate insisted on keeping back there. She was a workaholic, and often manned the shop even when sick, but didn't want to sneeze on anything.

Amber got a mask and pair of gloves out, putting both on a clean counter. Pulling her phone out of her pocket, she sent a quick text to Jessa. "Sending you some photos of the shop for insurance company before I try to straighten or clean-up." Donning the gear, she took her time with the photos, taking them from several angles. Once that was done, she set the phone back down on the counter and hit send.

Then she got to work. She started with the damaged glass case, cleaning the undamaged orbs and putting them safely on the back counter. Once all the product was cleaned off and moved, she began to work on the broken glass and dust. Amber lost herself in the task. Hours later, her back begged her to stop, and she glanced at the clock. The driver would be at the back door soon. Looking back around the room, she smiled. Except for the tiles in the mosaic and the case where the more expensive wands and orbs were displayed in, things were almost back to normal.

Pulling off the mask and gloves, she dropped them into a trash can and grabbed her phone again. One text from Jessa, thanking her for the photos. And one from Heath.

Amber leaned against the framework leading to the stockroom. Her muscles, already sore from cleaning, tightened even more at his name. *Nope, not ready to talk to you yet,* she thought and put the phone in her pocket with the message unopened.

She turned down the stereo. The buzzer was loud, but she wanted to be sure to hear it. Checking the clock, she decided to see what orders came in that she could pull, or at least have ready to do the next day.

Surprisingly enough, the store's email inbox was full of notes of encouragement. The community responded to the message she'd posted on the website with compassion and patience. She selected a few of the ones that touched her the most and started to print them off. She could drop them off at the hospital. Jessa would love to read them, and Amber read somewhere that comatose people could still hear. Maybe the support of her customers would help lure Kate's soul back.

"Who are you kidding," she muttered under her breath. "If her soul's with Charon, warm and fuzzy thoughts won't be what lures it back." She let out a heavy sigh and sat back in the chair. She'd promised Jessa she'd at least try to find a way. Her library at home was the best place to start. Amanda, her great-aunt, had compiled a large collection of books on Charon, Hades, and the Underworld. There was no way Amber could've been prepared to be Charon's Guardian, but at least the information was close by once she took on the role.

The doorbell rang, alerting her to the driver's arrival. It didn't take long to do the hand off. She locked the door again after he left. She collected the emails she'd printed off, stacked the order sheets neatly on the table for the next day, and went to turn off the computer. Two more emails sat in the inbox.

She scanned the first one. Nothing more than a sales pitch for web hosting services. The subject of the second one screamed at her. WHY DID YOU GO???!!!

Puzzled, she glanced at the return email. It seemed familiar, but she couldn't place it. Curiosity overrode her caution and she opened it.

Kate,

Why did you go in yesterday? I told you to stay away. I warned you both! Amber's safe and now you're not. She thinks she won, and I can't even come see you. I'm scared!

C.

The email she'd gotten late one night flashed in her mind. The spam she'd deleted. "Oh, no," she breathed quietly. She swung the cursor over to the junk box and clicked on it. The email she'd put there after the explosion was there. Same return address.

She pulled her phone from her pocket, dialing Larry's number with one hand while printing the emails with the other.

"Hello?" A female voice answered.

"Hi, Missy. It's Amber Cross. Is Larry available?"

"Sorry, Amber. He's not. He told me this morning he had to take care of something for a client in Caribou. He told me he won't be back until close to dinner time," his wife replied. "I can try to get a message to him if it's urgent. Cell coverage on the road is so spotty he just reroutes his calls here to the office."

"Yes, please. Could you ask him to swing by my place when he gets back in town? After he's eaten?"

"Will do, hon."

"Thank you." Amber hung up the call. It wasn't ideal, but at least she could do some research before he arrived.

Doublechecking that she had everything, Amber turned off the lights, went out the door, and locked it behind her.

Chapter Five

Amber dropped the empty cat food can into the trash and dashed upstairs. Pulling the chair away from the desk, she bent over the keyboard. A minute later, she found the email she'd delegated to the junk folder. Opening it up, she swore loudly.

Amber,

Don't go to work tomorrow. Keep Kate away, too. There's a package waiting for you both. Call the cops, don't touch it.

C.

A few more clicks and her printer hummed to life. As the machine spit out the paper copy of the email, she started to scan the titles on one bookshelf. Amanda was meticulous in how she'd kept the books, making it where all the books about Charon, Hades, and the Underworld were easy to find. Going through until she found a solution to get Kate's soul out wasn't going to be nearly as easy.

She selected the first half dozen volumes that felt right and put them on the small table next to her reading chair. She pulled her cell out of her pocket, put it on the charger next to the books, and dropped into the chair. Grabbing the top volume, she opened it up and started to scan the contents.

She shifted a bit as she read, but only when her body demanded it. No matter how much her muscles ached, she only got up to replace the books and collect others.

Sighing, she stretched a bit before settling back in. She had no idea how many books she'd gone through. She stopped counting over an hour ago. She settled back into the chair and pulled the next one off the pile. Opening the cover, she started the process again.

Her eyes narrowed as a phrase caught her attention as she skimmed through the book. Amber put a finger on the page, moving it as she read further. Hope started to rise in her soul.

A loud buzzing went off, making her jump. Blinking, she looked at her phone. The security camera for her front door showed Larry standing outside.

Deftly, she put a finger in the book to keep her place as she snatched at her phone with the other hand. "I'm upstairs," she answered through the intercom. "I'm unlocking the door. Meet me in the kitchen," she said.

She rose from the chair and grabbed a slip of paper off the desk. Placing it between the pages of the book, she freed her finger and closed it. Catching the printer out of the corner of her eye, she swiped at the printed email. She heard footsteps on the wood floor downstairs. "I'll be right down," she called out.

Turning off the lights, she darted out of the room and started to trot down the staircase. She heard Larry talking to someone. Slowing down, she waited to hear the reply. There weren't many people he'd let into her house easily, and she hadn't seen anyone else on the video feed.

Heath's laughter rang in her ears.

Well, she thought, *I guess we get to deal with that tonight, too.*

She started walking again, but this time kept her pace more measured. Larry didn't know they'd had a fight. This wasn't on him. But she was certain Heath had stood where he knew the camera wouldn't pick him up.

Minerva rubbed against her legs. "You can't be hungry," she told the cat. "I just fed you."

"Hey guys," she said as she walked into the kitchen. "I've got things to show you. Thanks for coming by, Larry." She placed the book and printed email on top of the stack she'd brought home from The Cauldron. "How was your trip?" she asked.

"Good, all things considered. I shouldn't have to make that trip again," Larry responded.

Bending down, she grabbed the cat's water bowl off the floor and started to rinse it out. "Glad to hear it. I know I'd be lost if I had to go somewhere with such spotty cell service."

"I brought pizza. Figured you'd be hungry." Heath said.

Amber began to fill the dish. "I'm good. Thanks." She placed the bowl back on the floor.

Turning back to her pile of papers, she said, "I was filling orders this morning. Mostly ones that had come in before the explosion. Took some photos for Jessa to submit to insurance, then cleaned up some. I needed to be busy. Sitting at the hospital wasn't going to do Kate any good, but cleaning up the damage would."

"How's she doing?" Larry asked.

Amber leaned against the counter and looked at him. "Not good. Physically, she should be fine. They were able to repair the damage to her body. But..." she paused.

"But what, Amber?"

She took a deep breath. "Her soul's gone. I went looking for it and it wasn't there." She shifted the papers in her hands. "When I was done cleaning the shop, I checked for new orders. I found a couple of emails that concerned me. Especially since I got one the night before from the same address." She handed the print outs to Larry. "I don't know who the address belongs to, or who 'C' is. But they tried to warn us both."

Larry spread the emails out across the kitchen island surface. "Did you share this with anyone else yet?"

Shaking her head, she said, "No. I printed them out and called you. Then came home and printed out the one I got."

"You said Kate's soul isn't there anymore," Heath spoke up. "What do you mean? She's brain dead?"

"No, nothing like that." Amber took a deep breath. "The powder in the blast was a mix of herbs. They're all part of a rare but powerful banishment spell. Whoever did it obviously didn't know how to cast it properly. If it had been, Kate wouldn't be in the hospital. One of the ingredients is something she's allergic to. Between that and how botched the casting was, it didn't motivate Kate to leave town. Instead, it forced her soul out of her body." She took another breath. "I know where it went, and how to get it back. I think. Larry, I'm going to be out of town for a few days or so. Would you take care of Minerva until I get back?"

She kept her focus on Larry but saw Heath shift on the edge of her vision. He wasn't happy. Probably planned to fight her on this. Hopefully, she could get Larry to leave before that happened.

Larry looked at her, shifted his gaze to Heath, then back to her. "No problem. I'll get the youngest on it. Text me a new code for the alarm before you leave if you change it. If you don't mind"—he started to stack the papers up—"I'm taking these with me. I'll show them to Sheriff Taylor, see if his cybercrime person can track down the owner of the email. Or at least if it was local or somewhere else." He glanced at the clock on the wall. "I've got to run, though. Promised Missy I'd grab some milk on the way back." He gave a direct look at Amber. "I know better than to talk you out of whatever it is you plan to do. There's too much of your great-aunt in you. And I don't need to know details. Just…be careful. We still have to discuss *your* will."

"I will be, Larry. Here, let me walk you out." She led him out of the kitchen and toward the front door.

"I'm sorry, Amber," Larry's voice was low. "I didn't know you and Heath were having problems or I wouldn't have let him in with me. He came up with the pizza right after you let me in."

"It's okay," she said.

They reached the front door and he put his hand on her shoulder before he opened it. "I know Bruce left scars.

Deep ones. Trust your instincts. If it's not feeling right, don't stay in a relationship because you're afraid of the fight. Good partnerships will have fights all the time. How you deal with them is what makes the difference." He glanced back down the hallway. "Changing your security code, though, is just practical if you're going to be gone for a while."

"Thanks, Larry." She smiled at him.

He winked at her. "If you run into Amanda, tell her I send my best." He pulled open the door and walked out into the night.

Amber closed the door behind him, a sense of calm coming over her. Larry understood what she had to do. Most likely, her great-aunt had done this at least once.

Turning, she took a deep breath. Heath probably wouldn't be nearly as accepting. *Too bad,* she thought, *because I gave my word.* She walked back down the hall to the kitchen.

Heath sat at the island, the pizza box lying open in front of him. "Need a plate?" she asked as she came into the room.

"Not really, since I'm the only one eating tonight." His voice had an edge to it.

"Suit yourself," she said. She grabbed a bowl out of the cupboard. Pulling open the fridge, she snagged a bagged salad mix and a few toppings and put those on the counter.

"If you wanted a salad, you could've said so before I came over."

She kept her back to him. "You didn't say you were coming over with pizza, either."

She heard the cardboard box slide across the counter behind her. "You haven't answered my calls or texts today, so how could I?"

"I was busy. Someone had to clean up the shop, keep orders going out." She finished putting her salad together and returned the ingredients to the fridge.

"And that had to be you?" She heard something in his voice. Was it exasperation? Disgust? Amber took a deep breath and shook off the feeling of dread. "If you 'have to keep the store open'," Heath continued, "what's going to happen when you go on this trip or whatever you were telling Larry about?"

"The orders are caught up. Most of the damage is cleaned up. Nothing else to really do now until Kate's awake and gives me some guidance. She might want to replace the tile mural over fixing it."

"Where do you think you're going to, Amber? You're not going to hunt down Kate's soul. It's either in her, or it's not. And that means she's dead. Whatever you told Larry is pure nonsense."

She turned, cradling the bowl in her hand. Stabbing at the contents with a fork, she said, "No, it's not. Her soul isn't in her body, but she's not dead. I know where her soul is. And going to get it is exactly what I'm going to do." Calmly, she took a bite.

"Jesus," he breathed. "What are you talking about?"

"Kate's in the Underworld," she said between bites. "Charon will come if I call him, take me to the Gates. I plead my need to Hades, gain entrance, and find her soul. Once we're back on my dock and we step foot off the ferry, her soul will return to her body. That's when she'll wake up."

Disbelief was written all over his face. "You're serious, aren't you? You really think you can pull that off? Go off with some mythical man to some crazy place that's a version of Hell and get her back? What if she's just gone, Amber? And her body's not figured it out yet? Or, say you 'find her' and she doesn't want to come back? Or you can't?"

She put the empty bowl on the counter next to her. "Charon will make sure I come back. He's as much my Guardian as I am his. I trust him to keep me safe."

"I don't."

"This isn't about you, Heath. It's not about me. It's about Kate. I'm the only one that can do this, and I'm going to do it." Her voice rose as she pounded a finger on the counter next to her. Anger was taking over. Why was he fighting her on this? "I don't know why you think this isn't worth doing."

Her hand bumped against the bowl and sent it crashing to the floor.

"Damn it," she swore as she bent down and started to pick up the shards. The edge of one piece caught her off guard and she sliced open a finger. "Shit," she swore again and put it to her mouth. Rising, she went to the sink and turned on the water.

As she stuck her finger under the faucet to clean the cut, Heath moved closer to her. "This is what I'm talking about, Amber." His voice was lower, calmer. He grasped her hand, moved it out of the stream of water, and wrapped a towel around it. "You can't clean up a broken bowl without cutting yourself. You don't have a clue where that thing will take you."

She looked up at him, "'Thing'?"

"You know what I mean. That… *thing,*" he gestured toward the rear of the house, "that drives the boat."

She pulled away from his grasp and stepped back, moving around the broken bits and away from Heath. "You're talking about Charon. He's a man, not a thing."

He tilted his head at her, his face changing. She couldn't quite read it. Was it jealousy? Fear? Disbelief? "I saw Bruce's body, Amber. There's no way a man could do that. A monster, possibly. But not a man."

"Let me make this clear, Heath. Charon is not a monster. He has a very specific job that he has to do. I gave

Bruce the same instructions I give everyone else who approaches. He chose to ignore them. That sealed his fate. Charon was only the instrument. Bruce earned his death."

"Amber, I know you didn't like him. Hell, he beat the crap out of me. I didn't mourn his death any more than you did. But nobody deserves to be shredded like he was. And nothing that has any real humanity in them could've done it. That thing's not human. He's a monster. One of these days, he's going to turn on you. Or one of our kids. Did you ever think about that? How you can possibly be Charon's 'Guardian' with a toddler on your hip?" He leaned against the counter, arms crossed. "You fulfilled the requirement for your inheritance. Sell this place, let someone else do the job, and start living a normal life for a change."

Her stomach dropped to her feet as she listened to him. He had her entire life mapped out in his head, without even asking her what she wanted. He'd never hurt her like Bruce had, but the control was the same. "Get out." She told him, her teeth clenched.

"You're not listening to me—"

"You're right. I'm not going to stand in my house and listen to you talk like that. I will do what I have to do to bring Kate's soul back. To make her whole again. And I don't need your permission to do it." She pointed down the hallway toward the front door. "Leave."

Angrily, he slammed the lid back over the pizza and picked it up. "Fine."

She stood there and watched as he stormed out of her house, slamming the door behind him. As soon as he was gone, she ran and locked it.

Turning, she slid down the wall. The control she'd kept came crumbling away. She'd sworn, once she'd left Texas, never to let a man even come close to controlling her. Never again. The fear she felt for Kate, the fight, all of it came crashing down on her. The sobs started.

She rode the tide of emotion, letting everything go. At some point, Minerva curled up in her lap. The shaking subsided, and she started to control her breathing again. She looked down at the cat. "You believe I can do this, right?"

The cat began to purr loudly and rubbed her furry face against Amber's.

Chapter Six
Waning Gibbous

Sighing, Amber looked over the items covering the workspace in the kitchen. Some rope, extra socks, a jacket, matches, protein bars, a folding knife with a hooked blade, and a small but well-stocked first aid kit. The pouch from the fireplace sat in the center. *Well,* she thought, *it's all within reason. Nothing here that the book said I can't take.*

She picked up the book from the counter and opened it to the bookmarked page. The summoning spell was simple, really. The list of items she would be allowed to take was sparse but easy to find around the house. Carefully, she began to put each piece into her backpack, separating things into different compartments as she could.

Minerva jumped up on the table and sniffed at the bag of coins. "I know," Amber said to the cat. "It's for a good reason. Even Amanda went once. Though her entry doesn't say whose soul she was trying to retrieve." The cat moved and began to worm her way under Amber's hand. Smiling, she scratched the cat's ears. "I'll be okay. Larry will come and feed you. I won't be gone long." She took a deep breath, "I hope."

Zipping up the last partition of the pack, she picked it up and tucked the book into a side pocket next to a small flashlight. Slowly, she put her arms through the straps and settled the pack on her back. Picking up the bag of coins, she looped the drawstring around her wrist. She took a deep breath and slowly released it.

"Well, Minerva. Everything's about as ready as I can make it. The alarm's been changed. Larry's got the new code. He'll be here to check on you until I get back, so no ambushes!" She teased the cat as she scratched her ears.

Her pocket vibrated. Puzzled, she pulled the phone out. One text, from Heath. *You don't know what you're doing.*

"Like hell I don't," she muttered. She went into the settings and blocked his number. Flipping the phone to silent, she placed it on the charging dock. "Not like I'll get service where I'm going," she said.

For a moment, her hand hesitated above the light switch. "I'll be back," she said. She didn't know exactly who she was talking to. The cat, the house, or herself.

She took another breath and found her center. She flipped the switch and strode toward the back door. Making sure the keys were secure in her pocket, she punched the code into the keypad. The alarm display beeped as it counted down the seconds she had to leave.

Not giving herself time to think about it, she twisted the doorknob and darted outside. Turning, she pulled out the keys and locked the door. Shoving the ring back into her pocket, she moved down the steps and crossed the patio.

The moon was just past full, but still brilliant enough to bathe the backyard in a gentle light. Stopping where she knew the dock would appear, she reached into the side pocket for both the book and flashlight. Clicking the button on the base, she aimed the beam at the book. Deftly, her finger found the marked page and opened it.

> *Charon, come and ferry your Guardian*
> *To the gates and Hades, I must go*
> *The soul of another is at stake*
> *Charon, come and ferry your Guardian*

She finished speaking and closed the book. Turning off the flashlight, she carefully placed both items back into the side of the pack. She folded her hands in front of her and waited. The only movement she made was a finger nervously stroking the silken rope. A stillness fell over the night. The gentle sound of the river lapping at the banks receded as the familiar fog moved in. Through the opaque clouds, Amber saw the dock begin to form. She took another deep breath and waited. Only when the platform was fully formed, and the swirling mist surrounded the yard, did she step forward.

She kept her gaze on the dark shape at the end. Charon and his boat were always the last to materialize. When she reached the end, she stopped.

He raised a hand and pushed the hood back. "You summoned me, Guardian? Why?"

Amber met his gaze and refused to back down. "There was an attack. I was spared, but a dear friend was not. Her soul has been forced from her body and resides in Hades' realm. I seek an audience with Him, to gain access to the Underworld."

Charon tilted his head, "You would find her soul and bring it back with you." He didn't ask.

Slowly, she nodded her head. "Yes," she answered.

His blue eyes stared at her. "What you ask is not easy. Hades does not often grant such favors. Not without payment of some kind."

Amber raised her chin. "My need is great. And Kate is worthy of the asking."

"Then come aboard, Guardian. And I shall take you to Hades."

Without hesitation, she strode the final steps to the end of the dock. Charon held out a hand to help her onto the craft. She looked at it and paused.

"You are my Guardian. And I am yours. There is no danger." His voice was even, reassuring her.

She placed her hand in his, surprised at the warmth it gave off. Using it to steady herself, she boarded the small boat and moved to the center bench. His words echoed in her mind. *"You are my Guardian. And I am yours."*

Turning, she sat down. Whatever was to come, she'd deal with it head-on.

The mist surrounded them, wispy waves that danced across the water and surrounded the boat. Charon moved the craft with great skill. The movement was fluid and continuous. She didn't even hear the water splash as he moved them forward.

This part wasn't what frightened her. Meeting Hades, convincing him to let her search for Kate's soul. That's where the true danger lay.

"You have questions, Guardian. You should ask them of me now."

Amber started a little as Charon's voice broke the silence around her. "I'm not sure what I need to ask yet." A nervous laugh escaped her lips. "I'm fairly certain you don't want me asking if we're there yet."

"Soon enough," he replied. "The journey is never as long as one anticipates."

"What's he like?" she blurted out.

"He is a God. His will in His realm is absolute. But He is not without reason. I don't know what your world has taught you of Hades. For some reason, many are surprised when they meet Him. Is He thought to be evil?"

She took a deep breath before answering. "I think it depends on the person. So many religions have maligned others, taken the Gods of old and turned them into something they aren't. For no real reason than to control new followers."

"Ah. That explains much."

Even surrounded by water and mist, Amber found herself at a comfortable temperature. It wasn't too hot or too cold. There was no wind, even though the fog swirled around them. "What moves the fog?"

"Many things. The breath of those who have ridden with me before. The thoughts of those who will be seated in my boat on the next journey. You do not feel it because you are still alive. For you, this trip will be a different experience from the one you will take with me later on."

"So, I'll ride with you again?"

"All ride my boat. Eventually."

The finality of his voice sent a chill down her spine. For just a moment, she wondered at the price Hades would ask.

"He will not ask that of you, Guardian. Your task is not complete."

She twisted in the seat, "He will not ask me to change places with Kate?"

"No. You are a Guardian. Until your successor is found and ready to take up the position, you are not going to remain in the Underworld. It is not possible."

"But Amanda...she died before I came to the house."

He looked down at her for a moment. The faintest hint of a smile played across his face. "She'd known where you were for some time. Had been watching you. The wait wasn't for nothing. You needed to have a way out, an escape. Until you reached that point, you would've resisted. Because of your parents, or because your tormentor wasn't there. The will had been drawn out and ready for a decade or more. She wanted to bring you here before she died. But that was not how it was to be.

"Amanda spoke of you to me often, Guardian. She was frustrated that she could not help you sooner."

"Charon, did she ever say what happened between her and my mother? I never asked her about it, the night I brought her to you. But I know something happened."

He raised his head and focused on the thick fog ahead of them. "Yes, but I cannot reveal what she said. The words spoken in trust by a Guardian remain sacred, no matter what." He paused, swinging the pole in his hands to the other side of the boat. "Be quiet, Guardian. The souls that live within Styx are restless."

Amber turned back to the front, her hands gripping the edge of her seat. The temperature began to drop as the fog grew thicker.

At first, it was barely a whisper that she could barely hear. As she concentrated, she started to hear the words.

"Charon carries a live one."

"Let us eat!"

"She will not pay the fare."

"You will join us."

"All join us."

"Take out your pentacle, Guardian!" Charon ordered.

Amber's right hand flew to the neck of her shirt and fumbled to find the chain around her neck. The voices rose, each one louder than the last. A cacophony of noise surrounded her.

She pulled the pendant out, surprised at how warm it felt at the touch. The emblem shone with white light. The glow began to envelop her.

"Almost, Guardian. You need to shield me and the boat as well. These creatures are hungry. They do not care on whom they feed."

Sensing the urgency in his voice, Amber closed her eyes and started to push the light out. It moved slowly, more because she feared tearing the fabric of the shield over anything else. Cries of anger and pain echoed in her brain as the creatures tried to push past the barrier. "These are the lurkers, aren't they? The ones who pull souls who try to get on without permission into the water?"

"Don't talk!" he snapped at her.

She kept her eyes closed, fighting the urge to react to the screams and shrieks that surrounded her. The boat began to rock violently, causing her to grasp the edge of the seat even tighter.

Waves of despair and sadness began to assault her. What was she doing? There was no way she could save Kate! Heath was right. This was a stupid idea! She can't do this alone! The light surrounding them began to fracture.

You're not alone, Guardian. You have never been. You have the strength to fight back. Charon's voice echoed in her mind.

Renewed by his faith in her, she pushed back against the negative thoughts. The light flared so brightly she drew back from it, even with her eyes closed. There was a crack of thunder that set her ears ringing. The boat stopped rocking, and the light faded.

"Well done, Guardian. Even Amanda would not have been able to do that."

Amber opened her eyes. The mist was gone. The water was calm once again. In the distance, she saw a single light. "What's that?" she asked, pointing at the horizon.

"The Gates to the Underworld," Charon replied. "Prepare yourself, Guardian. Hades awaits your arrival."

Chapter Seven

Heath tightened the last screw to secure the garbage disposal to the bottom of the sink. Grunting, he pushed himself out of the cabinet and stood up. "Go ahead and flip the breaker, Heidi," he called out. Reaching for the faucet, he turned on the water.

A loud click echoed from the laundry room. "It's live," Heidi called out to him.

Heath moved the switch on the wall and the mechanism roared to life. Turning it back off, he bent down and checked for leaks before turning off the water.

"You're all good," he said as he straightened back up.

"Great. That's been bugging me for weeks now. What do I owe you?" She reached for her purse.

"Nothing. You paid for the disposal. It's on the house."

Heidi placed a hand on her hip, "Now, Heath. I won't hear of it. You can't be doing things for free."

He wiped his hands on a towel, then started to put the few tools on the counter away. "I don't want to take your money, Heidi. You and the kids need that."

"The café's doing fine. And Roy had always said he was going to make sure we were well taken care of as long as he was active duty. We're fine." She pulled out some bills and folded them up before pressing them in his hand. "Don't need anyone thinking you were romancing an Army widow, now do we?" She laughed.

Heath shoved the cash into the back pocket of his jeans without looking at it. "Yes, ma'am," he replied with a grin.

"How about you bring Amber over for dinner tonight? I'd like to get to know her better." She leaned against a wall.

"She can't make it," he told her as he shut the toolbox. The sound of the lid slamming down surprised him. "She's, um, on a trip." Turning, he crossed his arms. "But I'm game if you want to entertain someone."

A phone rang, and Heidi pulled her cell out of her pocket. "Darn. It's the school again. Swing by at five?"

Heath nodded and grabbed the box off the counter. Waving at her, he walked out the back door.

Once in his car, he slammed his hand against the wheel. He hated covering for Amber.

No, it wasn't that. What he hated was she'd run off to do this without him.

Sighing, he turned the keys in the ignition. He'd go see Larry. Amber's aunt had leaned on him a lot. Some people said they'd had an affair at one point. Either way, Larry'd be the one person in town he could talk to about all this crazy stuff.

Easing out into traffic, he started driving to the lawyer's office.

***

"That was amazing, Heidi. You need to serve that at the café. You'd have them coming across the state." Heath told her as he placed his napkin on the empty plate.

"Not likely," Heidi laughed. "Come on, kids. Time to clean up."

Heath watched the twins as they moved quickly, removing the dishes. Although they were young, they each bore a marked resemblance to their father.

"Let's move to the living room, Heath. These two know what to do." Heidi rose from her seat.

Following his host, Heath moved to the other room. "Have a seat," she said, waving to an assortment of chairs and couches.

Sinking into a chair, he was surprised how comfortable it was.

He'd grown up with Heidi and Roy. But now found he was at a loss for words. They'd not said much of anything to each other since Roy's service. "The house looks good, Heidi."

She giggled, "Don't lie to me. You're no good at it. The house looks like crap." Moving to a small bar, she started to pour herself a glass of wine. "Want any?" She asked him.

"No, I'm good."

"Suit yourself." She set the bottle on the tray before heading to a couch. "I want to redecorate, get rid of this stuff," she waved her hand across the area before sitting down. "But the kids aren't ready. They got upset when I suggested we start packing up his office. I finally got his clothes out of my closet though." Leaning back, she took a drink. "Enough about me. I want to know what's really up with you and Amber. You just having fun, or is it serious?" She gave him a direct look over the rim of her glass as she took another drink.

Heath squirmed under the look. "I'm serious about it. Not sure she is though. I've got to be patient is all. She'll come around eventually."

"You? Patient? This coming from the guy who tried to figure out what was in the Christmas presents that sat under the tree at church every year?" She laughed.

"She's different, Heidi. She's not from around here. Doesn't have the same outlook the rest of us have. It's exciting."

"Exciting or not, Heath. Is it worth turning your back on everything you were raised to believe? You haven't been to church since she showed up. People are worried about you. Think she's cast some sort of spell on you."

He sighed, "Come on. It's not that bad. It's not like she's saying I can't go. I just…I don't know."

"You say she's out of town. When's she coming back?"

"I really don't know."

Heidi placed the empty wine glass on the coffee table, then curled her legs under her as she sat back down. "Listen, this is your business. The last thing I need to do is tell you what you should be doing. But she's gone off without you, doesn't say when she's coming back. Did she even bother to say where she was going? Or why?"

He ran a hand through his hair. "She did. I told her she shouldn't do it, not without me, but she went ahead anyway."

"So, she's running off without you. Won't tell you when she'll be back. Doesn't want you to go with her. Are you sure she's not seeing someone else?"

For a moment, Amber's face floated in his mind. The look she wore when she defended Charon to him. "I don't think so," he said. *But I don't know for sure*, he thought.

"Come out to the group tomorrow night. We're doing a mixer of sorts. Running the adult Bible study group at the same time as the youth group. That way, those of us with kids have someone to watch them. But we can still have time with adults."

For a moment, he hesitated. "Why not?" he replied. *It's not like Amber's around. She's off chasing some strange idea with a monster. Go have fun*, he told himself.

"Knock it off, Tamara!" Caleb, Heidi's son, yelled from the kitchen.

"I'll be right back," Heidi said as she rose from the couch.

Heath leaned back, trying hard not to eavesdrop on what was going on. The two kids were twins, but so different. Then again, it's not like Heidi and Jessa were even close to the same personality.

Was Heidi right? Could Amber be having an affair with someone else? He didn't like the idea, but it made more sense than the excuse she gave. That some creature from mythology showed up in her backyard every full moon and she had to escort souls onto his boat. That he couldn't see it because he wasn't a guardian or whatever, she said. The one time she let him stay there on a full moon was the night her ex showed up. After the beating he took from Bruce, Heath wasn't sure what he remembered of that night.

And whatever tore apart Bruce wasn't human. Or a bear.

Get a grip, he told himself. *What the heck could some mythical creature have that you don't?*

Then again, what could a handyman who barely made rent some months give a woman with a bank account larger than half of the annual operating budget of the state?

He needed a beer. Quietly, he rose from the chair. Heidi was still mediating the problem between her kids. He slid out the front door and left.

Chapter Eight

The glow grew, chasing away the darkness and fog slowly. Amber closed her eyes for a moment, intent on finding her center. She would need to stay calm, think quickly. Logic and intelligence would impress Hades. An emotional plea wouldn't matter.

"Prepare yourself, Guardian. We are here," Charon's voice alerted her.

Twisting, she saw him point in the distance. She rose, striving to keep her balance in the boat. "It's not what I expected," she whispered.

The dock thrusting out in the water was solid black, gleaming with a polished sheen. Behind them, opalescent gates towered into the sky. The upward slope of the dock ended at the double doors. No one was in view.

Charon skillfully maneuvered his boat and brought it even with the dock. Amber grasped at the pouch as it swung. Placing one hand on a pylon, she paused as she touched the smooth, cool surface. *You're not here to admire the architecture*, she chided herself. Stepping out of the boat, she slid the pack to the ground. Twisting the pouch off her wrist, she started to open it.

"Your journey is not done," Charon said, his voice low. "If you pay me now, you won't be able to return. Keep the coins in your pack, out of sight. You will need them later."

She nodded. Securing the drawstring, she knelt in front of her pack. Unzipping a small pocket, she shoved the bag inside it and shut it again. She rose, grabbing the straps as she did so. Once it was settled on her back, she started to walk up the ramp.

"Hold here, Guardian," Charon instructed her. Turning, she saw him loop a mooring rope around one of the pillars.

"You're coming with me?" she asked.

The closest thing to a smile she'd ever seen appeared on his face. "As I said, I am your Guardian as much as you are mine. This is my home. It is not right for me to simply leave you at the gates and walk away."

For some reason, his words reassured her. She wasn't going to be alone after all.

"Indeed, Charon's quite attentive to his duties when it comes to you, Amber Cross."

The deep voice, amused and curious, made her head snap around.

The gates were still closed, but they weren't alone anymore. A tall man, with dark hair and a full beard, stood within feet of her. His ice blue eyes bored into her soul.

A low growl alerted her. From behind the man, a dog padded forth. Each of his three heads zoned in on her.

That settled it. The man was Hades. No one else would be allowed that close to Cerberus.

She let loose a long breath and looked the god of the Underworld in the face. "My need is great," she started.

Hades held up a hand. "Please, Amber. No need for ritual phrases here. We're not that formal. Are we, my brother?"

"It depends on the guest," Charon replied.

Hades sighed, "Too true. I don't think this," he spread his arms wide, gesturing at the opulence of the gate behind him, "is quite what you expected, Amber. You're too much like Amanda. That one," he smiled, "chided me for such a display when she arrived. Enough of the niceties." He clapped his hands and rubbed them together. "You're here because your friend, Kate, lost her soul. Got it forced from her body. You want to take it back with you."

"You know?" she breathed, puzzled.

For a moment, the polite and jovial mask dropped and the true face of Hades shone through. Amber took a step back at the sight. "I'm a god, Ms. Cross. I know *everything*."

She felt a hand touch her shoulder, reassuring her. Hades smiled, but some of the mirth was gone. "Let's go have some breakfast, shall we? It's always easier to negotiate these things on a full stomach." Turning, with Cerberus at his side, he walked toward the gates.

Her insides shaking, Amber followed.

The doors disappeared as they approached, melting away into the first rays of dawn. A small, intimate dining room formed around them. Three chairs surrounded a table, a place setting for each of them.

"Grab a seat," their host called out. "Cerberus, come here,"

Amber stood, mesmerized as the details of the room came into focus. A fire blazed in a fireplace, close enough to make them comfortable. The room was cozy, inviting. A single portrait hung on one wall. Hades with a blonde woman. Persephone. A large pitchfork, taller than Hades himself, rested in the same corner as a large dog bed. Cerberus was curled up, each head gnawing on a bone.

"Sit, please." Hades motioned to the table once again. Amber glanced at Charon, who nodded slightly to her. She shrugged off the backpack and leaned it against a wall. Pulling out a chair, she eased herself into it.

"Good. You listen to his advice." Hades pointed a finger at Charon as he sat down. "Amanda didn't. Not at first. And it almost cost her."

A plate appeared in front of her. Steaming hot scrambled eggs. The bacon still sizzled. The crystal goblet in front of her filled with orange juice.

"Now," Hades said, stabbing at his eggs with a fork, "you're here to convince me to let you bring your friend, Kate, back to the mortal plane. Do you know who sent the bomb yet?"

Amber swallowed, regaining her calm. Picking up a fork, she said, "No, not yet. I believe in our system of justice. There's people who will find out who did this. I'm not a detective." She took a bite of the eggs, giving herself a moment to savor the taste in her mouth. Even Hugo's food wasn't this good!

"No, you're not. You're a witch." Hades replied. "Nothing wrong with that, but don't shortchange yourself. You were able to divine her soul was here, with me. Why not do the same to find the culprit?" He looked at her over the rim of his goblet.

"Because our laws are based on proof, fact, logic. The visions of a Wiccan wouldn't be admissible. I would know, yes. But hard evidence is what leads to convictions. Not blind faith."

"Still, you have your Guardian. He's gotten his hands dirty for you before. I believe his name was Bruce."

Amber looked Hades in the face. "Bruce refused my instruction and paid Charon a coin before he got on board. His fate was of his own making. Charon was merely the instrument of that doom. He wasn't acting on my orders." She sat up straighter, "I am a witch, yes. But I follow the Rede. I do no harm."

Hades leaned back, his face unreadable. Amber refused to back down from his gaze. She watched the god as his focus shifted to Charon and then back to her. The smallest hint of a smile played across his face.

"And so it was as you say." He leaned forward again, plucking a piece of bacon off of his plate. "Now, tell me. Why should I allow you to go into my realm to find Kate?"

Choosing her words carefully, she said, "Because the souls in your realm are judged on the life they led. Her life is not over. The one thing she was to learn during this turn of the Wheel may still be ahead of her. You are fair and just. You see the entire life a soul led, and base your decision on where they go on that. I don't believe you covet souls and enjoy torment. You're not the creature that modern faiths have turned you into. A wrong was done. One of the best ways to undo the wrong is to allow me entrance into the Underworld. To find her, bring her back with me. She'll enter her body once again, where she belongs, and the police will serve up a mortal justice."

"And what do you get, Amber? You're taking a huge risk. May have destroyed your relationship with your boyfriend because of it. What will you get, if I allow you to do this?"

She paused. Of all the questions she thought he might ask, this wasn't one of them. "I help my friend and her wife. I ease the pain Jessa feels by watching Kate lay in that hospital bed. Not dead, but not alive either. And I learn if that little girl I was when I came to Cavendish is finally gone. That I'm truly Amber Cross, and that my past is behind me." She stopped, stunned. Where did that come from?

Hades leaned back in his chair again, his face passive as he studied her. "I'm intrigued. That has to be one of the most honest answers I've ever heard to that question. Your great-aunt was a bit more blunt about her need. But she'd been a Guardian for longer than you by the time she came here."

"Who did she want to save?" Amber asked.

His eyes narrowed. "No. Not yet. If you don't have that answer before you leave here...then I'll tell you. But not yet."

"You'll let me find her, then?"

He nodded. "Yes, I will. You'll have full access to the Underworld. Find your friend, convince her to return if you can. But within a set of conditions."

"What are they?"

"Smart lady. You ask before you agree." He paused. "First off, you keep Charon with you at all times. He'd drive me nuts pacing if I tried to ban him from going with you.

"Second, you can speak to no one but Kate. Or Charon. With him, you can't start the conversation. He must. And you will respond truthfully and completely anything he asks you. If anyone else approaches you, you must remain silent while he speaks for you.

"Third, when you find Kate, you have five minutes to talk her into coming back with you. She may not want to. If, after that time, you haven't convinced her, you must retrace your steps and let her be. If she does come, you both must remain silent again unless Charon speaks to one of you first.

"Why?"

"The dead are drawn to the voice of the living. Especially the ones that don't accept their fate. They seek to enact vengeance on the living out of jealousy and spite. Charon will know where your voice won't be heard." He leaned forward again. "Do not say yes without considering all of this, Amber. Time is against you. The full moon was nigh on a week ago. If you are not back in your mortal world by the new moon, you will not return. No amount of pleading will save you. Your soul will be part of my realm, as will Kate's."

Amber took a deep breath and replied, "I accept."

Hades nodded. "I'm not surprised." He rose quickly. "Stay here. I need to send word to the Judges first. If Kate is before them already, your journey will be for nothing." He moved to a door that appeared in a wall. "You can rest in here. When I hear from them, I'll let you know." He pulled open the door.

Rising, she tried to see inside the room. It was dark and full of shadows. Her instincts screamed that something was wrong. This was too easy.

"No." She grabbed her pack and threaded her arms through it. "I appreciate the offer, but you said yourself that time wasn't on our side. We need to get started now. Not later."

The room began to spin and shift again as the god walked toward her. His face was stony. "You challenge me? I show you my hospitality and you dare refuse it?"

The walls solidified again, and she found herself in a small, circular room. There were no windows or doors. Only a small cot.

Her back was lighter. Alarmed, she realized her pack was missing. The jeans and shirt she'd been wearing were gone. Instead, she wore a dress of sorts. Two clips at the shoulders and a belt were all that held it to her body. There were no seams to it at all.

Charon was gone, too.

"Tell me, mortal. What would you do if I kept you here? Took my pleasure on your flesh? Kept a living woman as a trophy in a realm of undead as punishment?" He moved closer to her. "Perhaps I would summon Bruce and have him stay here with you when I couldn't."

She closed her eyes for a moment, intent on regaining an outward appearance of calm. Inside, though, she wanted to scream in terror with the threat. Opening her eyes again, Amber stared back at him, "Eventually, your wife would find me. She's known for making sure all is right when she comes home. And I would tell Persephone that the man who claimed to love her was unfaithful within months of her return to him." She raised her chin a little higher. "If this is the price you would demand to set Kate free, then I will pay it. But I don't think you're willing to let a way station go untended. I have not designated my heir yet. Too many souls would never find their way here. And then Persephone'd have to spend her time cleaning up your mess."

The walls shifted again, whirling faster than before. The effect threw Amber's equilibrium off, forcing her to her knees. Fighting against the waves of nausea, she focused on a single pebble on the ground and waited.

"Guardian? Are you hurt?" Charon was next to her.

She took a deep breath. Her clothing was back to normal. The weight of her pack rested on her back.

She shook her head. Sitting back on her legs, she looked around her. The room was gone. A barren, rocky plain stretched out on all sides. Relief flooded through her. Hades hadn't called her bluff.

"Good," Charon replied. "Come, we must move. This place is not safe." He held out a hand to her.

Taking his hand, she let him help her get up. She wanted to ask where they were, but Hades' warning rang in her mind. There was no way to know if he lied, but she didn't feel like testing the theory.

Nodding once to Charon, she followed him and began the trek to find Kate.

Chapter Nine

"Seth said my car should be ready later today," Kate said as Jessa eased the car up to the curb in front of The Cauldron.

"No worries," Jessa replied as she put the car in park. "My next trip won't be until next month. Cavendish isn't so big we have to have two cars." She laughed.

Kate leaned over and gave her wife a kiss. "Plus, I get one more kiss this way." She opened the door and stepped out. "Amber should be in later. I can have her close up tonight if you want to catch an early show."

"I can't. Got a client scheduled at five."

"Okay. Love you!" Kate shut the door. Turning to the door to her shop, she spied a box sitting on the welcome mat. Curious, she picked it up. There wasn't a return address, but the handwriting looked familiar in some way. *Probably a return*, she thought. as she tucked it securely under one arm. With the other hand, she unlocked the door and stepped inside.

Using one foot to make sure the door shut behind her, she put the package on the round display table in the center of the room. As she placed her cell phone and wallet down, she picked up the box to examine it. There wasn't a postmark. *That's odd*, she thought. Her mind started to think about her local customers. Who lived close enough to drop it off? And why not wait until she was open? Puzzled, she used her keys to break the tape around the edges of the box.

Searing pain crashed through her body as the contents exploded in her face. Screaming, she fell to the ground. And that's when the pain got even worse.

The center of her being was burning, driving her soul from her body. She clawed at the tethers, desperate to stay. This wasn't death. It was eviction.

Her soul flew out of her body and she saw herself, crumpled and bleeding, on the floor of her shop. The mosaic tiles broken and dusting her body. A silent scream escaped her ghostly form as everything went black.

When she woke, she took a deep breath. Her hand flew to her chest. She could still feel her heart beating. *Good. I'm not dead. Not yet, anyway.*

The ground beneath her crunched as she rolled over. The area was littered with sharp rocks, too small to be gravel. She winced as a pointed one dug into her knees and palms as she pushed herself upright.

Think, Kate. Don't react. Think.

Carefully, she turned around and took in her surroundings. Judging by the amount of light, she figured it was daytime. But there was no sun in the sky, no clouds, for her to estimate a time.

The rocky expanse stretched far into the horizon in three directions. To her left, a series of small hills dotted the landscape. It was a better option than some place with absolutely nowhere to hide. Resolutely, she set out for the area.

Okay, first things first, she thought. *Find shelter, water. Then figure out where you are.* She sighed. *Scratch that last one. You know where you are. And it's not Cavendish.*

She started to piece together things as she walked. Her soul had been forced from her body. By someone who really didn't know what they were doing. Someone local enough to put it at the store for her to find over sending it through the mail.

There was something familiar about the handwriting, too. But she wasn't sure what. The style was simple. Block letters, not cursive. Nothing distinctive about it. Still.... she felt like she should know who wrote it out.

Reaching the top of a small hill, she crouched down. Caution told her to wait, see what could be seen before revealing herself.

A river, wide enough that the other bank wasn't visible, cut across the valley below. To her right, a massive wall. The black beach wasn't covered in sand. If anything, it looked like a smooth sheet of obsidian. A pier rose up from the ground, jutting out into the water. Two figures stood to the side. Male, from their height and build. One had his head covered by a hood. The other absently scratched the ears of the middle head of the dog at his side.

"Shit!" Kate swore, ducking her head down as Cerberus' heads turned toward her position.

She bit her lip, staying quiet and waiting for the panic to pass. That confirmed it. She was in Hades' Underworld. The only thing that could save her now, get her soul back to her body, was having someone from the mortal plane coming to get her.

Or convincing the Judges to send her back. *Not likely,* she thought. None of those three had a reputation of granting a return. Their job was to determine if you made it to Elysium. Or somewhere else.

Making as little noise as possible, she started to make her way back down the hillside. Her only hope now was to stay hidden and wait.

But who would even be able to come here and find her?

The still air was broken by a piercing howl. Turning her head toward the sound, Kate spied several small figures in the distance. The movements were jerky, disjointed. The howling echoed again. *Don't just sit there,* she scolded herself. *Move, damn it!*

***

A small bead of sweat ran down Kate's face. Whatever those things were, she lost them. Or, rather, hoped she did.

The cave was dark. There was water in here. She could smell it. Steadying herself, she took a few deep breaths. Then listened. The baying of the creatures was retreating. Good.

She made her way deeper into the cave, moving as silently as she could. Until she knew was the only occupant, she wasn't going to let her guard down.

The tunnel stopped, opening up to a cavern so large she couldn't see the other side. Or the bottom, for that matter. Making out a small outcropping of rock, she hoisted herself onto the ledge. It was mostly hidden, and had only enough room for her to lay down on.

In other words, defensible.

Sliding down the wall, she sat on the ledge. So much had happened. Her mind shied away from comprehending everything at once. *Okay,* she told herself. *One thing at a time. There's no way to solve the whole puzzle. Gotta look at one piece at a time.*

She was in the Underworld but could feel her heart still beating in her chest. Her body wasn't dead. Point in her favor.

But that also made her a target. Wayward souls were hunted, driven to cross all the rivers and face the Judges. The cave would keep her safe for only so long.

Think, Kate. You're not going to survive if you don't.

Given the gate and Cerberus, that first river had to be Styx. The man next to the dog must've been Hades. Which would make the other one…what? A soul coming to His realm?

Her eyes flew open wide. No, the relationship was too familiar. They had the stance of two men talking shop. Which meant the hooded figure was probably Charon.

Amber!

Closing her eyes, Kate found her center again. *Amber, if you can hear me, come find me. Please!*

A wave of exhaustion washed over her. She curled up and let it take over.

Chapter Ten

Amber bit her lip for what felt like the fiftieth time since they'd started walking. Her mind whirled with questions she wanted to ask but knew not to. *Trust Charon,* she told herself. *He'll tell me when it's safe, allow me to ask a few questions. I hope.*

The rocky plain gave way to grasslands. Her hand brushed against the top of the blades as she walked next to her Guardian. That's how she thought of him, now. She no longer guarded him. The tables had turned.

His hand landed on her shoulder, making her stop. "There," he said, pointing to the horizon. A small wisp of smoke rose into the perpetual dusk. "We will be safe there tonight."

She glanced at his face, nodding. *Like I can argue,* she thought.

"You could, Guardian. But I do not advise it." Charon replied, a hint of humor in his voice.

Smiling, she moved into step with him. She'd forgotten he could read her mind. That would make it easier, she hoped, to get answers later on.

"Not always, Guardian. Surface thoughts you give away through your face and movement. The deeper ones…those I cannot read." He hesitated. "Hades instructed you to answer all questions I have, fully and truthfully. I hope you won't find any of them to be overreaching, Guardian. I haven't had the chance to learn of your plane for some time. And your world changes at a rapid pace."

She took a deep breath and released it. It did make her feel better, knowing he wouldn't be able to read everything on her mind. No matter how much she tried, the fights she'd had with Heath before leaving kept replaying themselves in her head. Was she overreacting to his words? Or were they simply wanting different things from life?

Ten minutes or so later, a small house came into view. The spiral column of smoke Charon had pointed out continued to form out of the chimney that peeked out of the thatched roof. Flower boxes, full of plants, sat below the windows. A single wooden door stood in the center of the stone structure.

Amber hung back, giving Charon the lead. Until she knew what was in the cottage, she wanted to stay out of sight.

"No need for caution, Guardian. The one that lives here will not harm you." He turned and smiled at her.

Beyond him, she saw the door open. A figure stood in the threshold. Amber's eyes widened with surprise and relief.

"Welcome to my new home, Amber," Amanda called out. "Come inside before all the heat escapes." Her great-aunt motioned them forward with a wave of her arm.

A sudden chill descended over Amber's body. Glancing up at Charon, she saw him motion her forward with his chin. Her step quickened and she entered the house.

The one room was lined with shelves filled with hundreds of books. A single bed rested near enough to the fireplace to keep the occupant warm but not overly so. Overstuffed chairs and small tables were scattered everywhere.

"Welcome, Amber." Amanda opened her arms, ready to embrace her.

Amber glanced at Charon again, hesitating. "This is a safe place, Guardian. While the other geas are still upon you, no harm can be done on you here."

She all but ran to Amanda, relieved to find a friendly face. "What geas, Charon? And why is she here?" Amanda's voice throbbed through her chest as Amber embraced her.

"She is here because she summoned me. One that is dear to her was harmed, her soul sent here before their time. Amber convinced Hades to let her try to find it."

Amber felt Amanda's hands grasp her shoulders and break them apart. "Whose soul?" she demanded.

Amber swallowed hard, not wanting to say anything.

"Kate's," Charon answered for her.

"Why are you speaking for her?" Amanda demanded.

"One of the conditions Hades put on her was that she could not speak to any but Kate when we found her. Or to me, and then only to answer a question posed by me. She isn't answering because she is forbidden to do so."

A dark cloud moved across Amanda's face. "That's ridiculous. How does Hades expect her to hold to that?" She moved away from Amber. "Sit, my child."

Gratefully, Amber sank into one of the chairs while Amanda moved two others closer. "If I've got to go through you," she pointed at Charon, "to talk to my heir, so be it. I hope you're ready."

Charon smiled slightly. "Would it be possible to feed her first?" he asked, waving at Amber. "She has had nothing since Hades gave her breakfast."

"Well, that's hardly being a good host. He should've done more to make her ready for this trip." The older woman found a bowl and moved toward a small pot resting near the fire.

"Amber, do you feel Hades mistreated you?" Charon asked.

She took a deep breath as the compulsion to stay silent lifted from her. "Not in the sense of feeding me, no. His threat terrified me. If I didn't love Kate as I do, I wouldn't have had the courage to stand up to Him."

Amanda spun about. "He threatened you? How? So help me Goddess, I will make Him pay if he harmed you! I don't care what He is!"

Charon looked at her. His face was different. Was that compassion? Fear?

"Guardian, how did he threaten you? I never left your side and heard no threats."

"When I hesitated going into the one room and told Him we had to start the journey, Hades did…something. I don't know what. The room spun and shifted. I was in a windowless room. Nothing but a single bed. My clothing was different, and my pack was gone. You weren't there. He threatened to keep me there for refusing His hospitality." She paused. "He threatened to rape me, keep 'a living woman as a trophy'. To have Bruce there with me when He couldn't be." She shifted in her chair. "I was scared, terrified. But I also knew that, if this was the price he demanded to get Kate free, I'd pay it. Then I remembered something I read in the library. About how Persephone would spend days going about the Underworld to find out everything Hades had been doing since her last visit. I took a gamble, said I'd have no hesitation to tell her everything He'd done to me. Next thing I knew, I was on my knees on a rocky plain and Charon was next to me again."

Amanda thrust a bowl in her hands. Steam rose from the contents as Amber's hands warmed up. "Eat," her great-aunt commanded her, the tone gentle and loving over chiding. "Charon, I'm getting you a bowl as well. Don't argue." She pointed a finger at him as she went back to the kitchen area.

"I wouldn't dream of it, Amanda," he replied.

"If you haven't figured it out yet, Amber, Charon here is full of common sense. More so than you or I. When he's with you, listen." The older woman brought another bowl out. "You'll regret it if you don't."

Amber smiled, scooping a spoonful of the stew and bringing it to her mouth. She had so many questions! Where were they? Why was Amanda here? Why hadn't she faced the Judges and moved on to Elysium? And would she ever tell her whose soul she came to retrieve decades ago?

To keep herself from asking, she kept eating. The other woman studied her, but her gaze moved over to Charon more than once.

"Was any prohibition made against her writing things down?"

Amber's eyes widened. She looked over at Charon, a bit of hope springing in her.

He kept his deep blue eyes focused on her. "Not that I remember, no. It was verbal communication that He limited."

"Let's test it." She rose from the chair and moved to a small table in a corner. "Amber, I can see you're full of questions. It's all over your face. Write one down, and hand it back to me. I'll read it and give you the answer. As long as there's no reaction from outside, we're good."

Charon turned, "The risk is too great. You could alert the Hounds to where she is!" He started to rise out of his chair.

"Sit down, Charon. Do you really think I'd risk the notice of those things?" She crossed to Amber, holding out a pencil and pad of paper. "Besides, this place is too well warded. She can't speak. That's been prohibited. But writing wasn't."

Amber hesitated, carefully placing the empty bowl on the table next to her. She looked over at Charon.

"I believe she's right, Guardian. I think this is safe. At least, here it is. And it will speed things up if I don't have to guess at what you want to know."

Reaching out her hand, she grabbed the items. Taking a deep breath, she wrote her first question. Tearing off the top page, she handed it to her great-aunt.

Amanda moved the chair closer and sat down, reading the paper. "You're in my home, but you knew that. You're on the second island of the Underworld. This place is built as rings, separated by rivers. There's only one between where we are and where you got off Charon's boat."

"Lethe," Charon said.

Amanda nodded, "Yes."

Furiously, Amber scribbled a few more questions Tearing the page off, she all but shoved it into Amanda's hand.

"I'm still here, child, because I choose to be. I could move on, yes. But I'm useful. When souls have crossed Lethe, they often lose their way. Fall into a madness of sorts. I comfort them, let them know all will be well, and prepare them for the next stage of the journey. Not all come to me. Few do, to be honest. But Kate hasn't, which is good. I'd know if she had gone past me. But now I have a question. How did her soul come here? And why do you come after it?"

Amber chewed her lip, trying hard not to speak. It was going to take time to write everything down.

"Guardian," Charon interrupted her thoughts. He knelt in front of her, his face impassive. "I sense you feel you cannot write the events down. There is another way, if you allow it. It will not hurt. I will never do anything to bring you harm. If you allow me to be a bridge, I can see into your mind. Learn what happened to bring you here. I can pass that information to Amanda."

Amber started to open her mouth, and he held up a hand to silence her. "Do not agree so quickly, Guardian. To allow me into your mind like this…you cannot keep things hidden from me. You would need to go to the moment this tangle began and I would know everything from that moment to this one. I will not share it all with Amanda, nothing will go to her other than as it applies with why you search for your friend. I will still know it all, though. Think before you agree."

She took a deep breath, her mind racing through everything that'd happened in the last few days. The attack, finding the spell, the fights with Heath. And then she realized there wasn't anything there that she wouldn't want him to know about. She met his gaze again, nodding once.

"Do you agree to this, Guardian?"

"Yes, Guardian," she replied.

"Then close your eyes and focus on when this tangle began." He reached one hand and placed it on top of her head.

She did as she was told, keeping her breathing as regular as she could. She went back to being woken up by her phone ringing. How it kept ringing the morning of the explosion. Something else, warm but strange, began to flow around her mind. Charon's presence wormed into the folds of her memories, an avid watcher as the recent events were relived for his viewing. Every minute detail became amplified. The shock of the news. Pain and confusion about Heath. The softness of Minerva's fur. And her own determination to bring Kate back.

She thought he'd retreat once she got to the memory of summoning him, but he didn't. He stayed in her mind, forcing her to relive her doubt of her abilities to keep the lurkers at bay. The terror she felt when Hades suggested letting Bruce be alone with her in that sealed off room. And the relief that her bluff had worked when she saw Charon again.

At last, his mind retreated from hers. She became aware of herself again. Her entire body shook in a way she couldn't control it. Her face was wet with tears she didn't know she'd shed.

"Oh, my child," Amanda's voice came from in front of her. Amber opened her eyes. Her great-aunt sat in front of her, gently pushing damp hair away from her eyes. "I can't imagine ... Come, you need to rest." She let Amanda pull her out of the chair, her body still shivering uncontrollably. "You sleep. Charon and I will come up with a plan while you do. We will help you find Kate."

The bed she was led to was surprisingly soft. Slipping off her shoes, she fell onto it. The blanket Amanda draped over her was warm and soft. Before she drifted off, she searched for Charon. He was back in his chair, watching her. The impassive face was marred by the clenching of his jaw. *Was that a tear*, she thought? But sleep took hold of her and she didn't fight it.

Chapter Eleven
Third Quarter

When she woke, the house was quiet. Only the occasional crackle and pop of the log as it burned in the fireplace. Shadows danced across the walls.

Amber moved the blanket off of her and sat up. She didn't see either Amanda or Charon. She found her shoes and started to unlace them. She couldn't hear any voices. Wherever they were, it wasn't in the room with her.

Once her shoes were back on and tied, she rose from the bed. The room hadn't changed since she'd gone to sleep. The chairs were still in the small circle. Two bowls sat near the sink, ready to be washed. The echo of the latch dislodging on the door sounded. Amber turned, facing the door. Amanda entered, closing the door behind her.

"Oh, you're awake," she commented as she placed her shawl on a peg near the door. "I thought you'd be asleep awhile longer."

Relieved, Amber started opening her mouth. Shutting it quickly, she grabbed the pad of paper and pencil. *Where's Charon?* she scribbled. Ripping off the page, she handed it to Amanda.

"He's trying to pinpoint Kate for you. Between the two of us, we were able to get a general idea where she might be. Hades gave you a time limit, though, so Charon decided to narrow the search a bit more. He didn't want to waste time going in the wrong direction." She crossed to the fire. "Want some tea? Or something a bit stronger?"

Amber didn't respond, just watched her. Something wasn't right. She didn't know Amanda well, that's for certain. The woman had died before she even knew she existed. But her mannerisms were off.

"Well, I need something stronger right now." The older woman took a deep breath and let it out as she rummaged through the cupboards. "Have a seat, Amber," she called out. "Charon's insisted that you and I have a chat. Or, rather, that I spill some secrets. Ah, there it is." She pulled a dark green bottle from the cupboard. Turning around, she slowed down as she reached for a glass. "Please, sit. I'm going to have a hard enough time with this. I don't want you glaring down at me. And make sure that pencil and pad is nearby. I'm certain you'll have questions before I'm done." Amanda said as she crossed to the small arrangement of chairs.

Amber sank into one of the chairs. Placing the pad and pencil in her lap, she folded her hands and waited. Curiosity ran rampant through her veins. What could Amanda possibly tell her that is so important that Charon would insist on it?

Twisting the cork loose, Amanda poured a liberal amount of amber-colored liquid into the glass. She put the bottle on the small table next to her chair and sat down, glass in hand. "Not nearly as good as what you've got back at the River House," she commented as she looked at the contents of the glass. "But it'll serve the purpose." She raised her arm, "Here's to family skeletons finally coming out of the closet," she said. In one swift motion, she downed the contents.

"Your grandmother and I were twins. Not identical in the least bit. Especially once you got to know us. She got all the beauty. Fair hair and skin, slender build, everything that was popular back when we were born. I preferred climbing trees and building forts over playing dolls. And forget about how I looked. I gave up trying to be beautiful next to her. I didn't resent her. She was the other half of me. But the feeling wasn't mutual.

"When we turned eighteen, she got engaged to your grandfather. And I was visited by a lawyer about a strange inheritance. None of us knew the person who left me the River House. It wasn't a relative at all. But I was eager to experience life as a woman of means, one that didn't have to listen to what her husband said. I moved in the day after her wedding.

"I found out about Charon and the rest of it a few weeks later. It took some getting used to, that's for sure. My sister and her husband came and visited me a few times. I think she envied me. I couldn't be sure, but I don't think the marriage was all she thought it would be. When he got a job in Texas, we settled for occasional letters. I lived my life, and she lived hers.

"By the time your mother was born, I had found Wicca. Had given myself over to the faith. Created the space in the attic so people wouldn't come over for a party and stumble across my secret. I still had to hide it, back then. It's one reason I never fell in love with someone else. I loved the freedom the money gave me. The ability to travel where I wanted to as long as I was home for the full moon. People in town thought of me as eccentric, but harmless. I lived life on my terms, not theirs. But I knew I had to find my heir as well.

She poured another shot of whiskey but didn't drink it as fast. Instead, she kept her head down. Whatever she was about to say was important. Amber shifted in her seat, listening closely.

"I knew, somehow, that my heir would come from my sister's family. Had for years by the time your mother was born. I honestly thought it would be her. I started to write and call more. When your mother was twelve, I invited her to spend the summer with me. I wanted to meet her, see if she was someone who could shoulder the burden of being Charon's Guardian.

"When she arrived, I knew she wouldn't be strong enough. Your grandparents were very religious, and she'd been thoroughly versed in the dogma connected with their church. I'm not saying that's wrong." Amanda put her hand up. "But, as you know, it would've caused a problem when the full moon came. If a Guardian were to ever turn away from the burden, sell the house.... souls would wander the world, lost. When it comes time to select your own heir, Amber, watch them first. Make sure you know they'll not run from the responsibility."

Amber nodded in understanding. For a moment, she imagined how her mother would've reacted to even the idea of Charon or guiding souls. She shuddered. It wasn't a pleasant image.

"Anyway, I'd promised her a whole summer. I still was certain my heir would be connected to her in some way, and I was determined to become enough of a presence in her life to stay part of it. In case it was her child, or one of her friends. She had the run of the house. The only places I banned her from were the library and my room. One because of what books were in there. The other because I didn't want her finding the attic.

"I'd gone to the store. We'd run out of milk." Amanda's voice got a dreamy quality to it as she recalled what happened. "When I got back, I couldn't find her. I went upstairs and heard her running. She'd gone into the attic. I saw her come out of my bedroom. Her face was white, she was in shock. All she knew of Wicca was that it was evil, the devil's work. She started to scream at me in fear. I tried to reason with her, but she was so scared. She tried to run past me. I grabbed her hand, begging her to calm down. Let me explain. She jerked away and tripped, falling down the stairs."

Amber leaned back in her chair, shocked. Tears ran down Amanda's face as she looked at her. "I didn't push her. I didn't want her to be hurt. But she landed by the front door with a sickening thud. I panicked. She had to live in order for my heir to be found. I took her body into one of the spare rooms and laid it out. That night, I summoned Charon and told him the story, compelled him to take me to the Underworld. To convince Hades to let me bring her soul back."

She took another long drink. "He relented, as you know. But your mother…she wasn't sure she wanted to go back. Hades gave her an illusion of the Christian heaven. I had to promise her that I'd give her a lot of money when I died. She wouldn't leave until I swore to it. And then Hades brought down the illusion, made sure she saw the Underworld for what it is. He made her meet Cerberus. This is why your mother hated me, cut me out of her life. Because Hades made sure she remembered everything that happened. And He made me agree to forgo my own eternal rest. I will remain here, and listen to the souls that come to me, but I'm forever in limbo."

She took a deep breath, her entire body shuddering. "When I drew up my will and named you as my heir, I put her in it. Granting her the sum I'd promised her and not a penny more. But I stipulated that she couldn't contact you unless you initiated it. And couldn't tell anyone where you'd gone. Larry has an envelope in his office. Photographs, things she did before she met your father. Things she's terrified will be made public. I made her a promise, and I kept it. But I made it clear that the money wasn't without strings. It may have been wrong of me. But I only sought to protect you."

Blinking, Amber looked at the floor. Her mind frantically tried to process Amanda's words. Now she knew why her mother never mentioned her. Or her grandmother. Fleeting memories of photos albums with torn photographs inside skittered across her brain. Her hands gripped the pad and pencil tightly. So many questions! Furiously, she scribbled one and ripped the page from the pad before handing it to Amanda.

The older woman took it. Amber saw her hands shaking as she read it. "How much did I pay for you?" she whispered. Amber's heart raced as she stared at Amanda.

Crumpling the page, she locked eyes with her. "I didn't pay anything for you. You've always been free to walk away. You still are. But, to answer your question, your mother demanded not a penny less than $500,000. Even at the age of twelve, she was shrewd. Insisted that she be given the money regardless if you were my heir or not. And also commanded me to stay out of your life until I died. The day after we returned, I called Larry to the house. Made the change in my will right in front of her. When he left, she gave me the coldest smile I'd ever seen on a person, regardless of age." She raised a hand to her face and angrily swiped at the tear running down her cheek. "When he was gone, she told me she planned to raise you in such a way that you'd never question her authority. Get you married off early, stay in town, and obey her. That, should I actually name you as my heir, that you'd never set foot in the house. You'd sell it and make her guardian of your fortune. She took a small Bible out of her pocket, held it up, and swore to me that my 'sinful ways' would never influence you. Five or six years ago, I got a letter from her. She demanded the money I'd promised her. Said she'd talked to someone in town, convinced him to date you. That she'd pay him part of her inheritance if he married you." Her voice shook, but Amber couldn't tell if it was from anger or something else. "I didn't buy you, Amber. But she sold you to Bruce. For ten percent of what she would inherit."

Amber's stomach dropped. Her own mother sold her? Made a deal with Bruce like she was some piece of property? Fragmented memories formed in her head. Of looks exchanged between her mom and Bruce. The constant push for marriage. It started to make sense.

Rising from her seat, she knelt in front of Amanda. She took the glass from her hands and put it on the table. Turning her palms up, she gently kissed the wrist of each one. Amber looked at her great-aunt's face and slowly mouthed the words, *I forgive you.*

The house and everything disappeared around her. A hand appeared in front of her. Looking up, Amber saw Charon, waiting to help her up. "You've done well, Guardian. Amanda has been released and goes to Elysium now."

Amber put her hand in Charon's and rose. The featureless plain surrounding them once again. Her mind whirled with questions. "Not yet, Guardian. When we rest tonight. But you might need those." He pointed to the ground at her feet.

A pad of paper and pencil sat there, waiting for her to pick them up.

Chapter Twelve

Charon raised his hand above his eyes, shading them from the sun, and looked back. Amber wasn't far behind him. Her shoulders slumped. And her hands didn't grip the straps of her pack nearly as tightly as they had before. She was tired.

"There's a safe spot to rest not far from here, Guardian." He kept his voice even as she closed the gap between them.

She nodded, pausing long enough to rest her hands on her knees and catch her breath.

He hated to push her like this. In truth, Hades would've preferred he'd driven her even harder. That he took the detour and let her meet with Amanda…Charon would have to answer for that later.

She was tougher than Hades gave her credit for. Not a single word had passed her lips. It was hard for her, and he could see that. He'd been thinking of what she might want to know, trying to anticipate her need for answers to questions she couldn't ask.

The meeting with Amanda was bound to top the list. Especially after Amber had done the one thing Charon had hoped for. She'd forgiven her, unconditionally. The condition that caused her to be bound to that spot lifted. Amanda, his friend and Guardian for close to eighty years, had finally gone before the Judges and deemed fit to move on to Elysium.

He missed her.

Amber stood upright, nodding to him. She was ready to move again. "We can rest for the night in there," he pointed to the craggy hillside nearby. "There's a cave. It's safe."

One of her hands clenched in a fist, the thumb raised up. Charon began the short hike to the trail cut into the jagged earth.

Moving quickly, he listened for any sound. She was abiding by Hades' rules, but that didn't guarantee He wouldn't change them.

That's not the only concern you have, he chided himself.

Delving into Amber's mind the night before haunted him. It wasn't just the scars she still bore from what Bruce had done to her. There was so much more pain than he expected. And the complexity of emotions she had when it came to the other man, Heath, had him truly puzzled. He didn't want to add to her discomfort, but he'd have to ask her some questions tonight. For both his curiosity and her safety. The ferryman they'd have to deal with crossing the River Lethe was sly. She'd face a temptation like no other.

And so would he.

Resolutely, he pushed the jumble of thoughts and emotion from his mind. He was her Guardian right now. He had a job to do. He had a good idea where Kate was. The link gave him enough information to get close enough to her that they should find her and get back to his boat well before Hades' deadline. And then he could spend a brief time in the mortal world. Until the attacker was found, he would guard her. He wasn't convinced that the target was Kate.

Glancing up, he spied the opening he'd been looking for. "There," he said, turning to Amber and pointing to the spot. "We rest in there tonight."

Relief flooded her face. She placed her hands on the jagged rocks around them, using them to help her body move forward.

Turning back around, Charon climbed the last of the trail and got to the mouth of the cave. The light didn't penetrate far. There was enough, though, for him to know it was empty.

Of course, it's empty, he thought. *How many other mortals are in the Underworld, seeking one they love? Or hiding from Hades?*

He was Charon, ferryman for the River Styx. He knew the answer was none. Because only Amber had cared enough to summon him.

"No one else is here," he told her as she reached the entrance. "We'll need light, but the resting spot isn't far inside."

She smiled at him. Shrugging the pack off her shoulders, she unzipped a section and rummaged in it. Pulling out a black cylinder, she handed it to him.

Turning it over in his hands, he tried to figure out what it was. It was made of metal and solid black, except for one end that was lined in silver, with a clear cover protecting a small object inside. He looked at her, puzzled.

Smiling again, she finished getting the pack settled on her back again. She took the rod from his hand and touched it on the shaft. A beam of white light shone from the clear end. She handed it back to him. It was cool to the touch, no heat radiated from it. Curious, he asked, "What is this?"

Amber touched her fingers to her lips and looked at him questioningly.

"It's safe here. Again, what is this?"

"It's called a flashlight. There's batteries inside that give power to the bulb, creating the light." Her voice was soft, with a slight rasp to it. Then again, she hadn't used it since the night before. She looked up at him and sighed. "It's not something I can explain easily. Just press here" — she touched a spot on the device— "and you'll see."

He did as she instructed. A beam of light shot out of one end, illuminating the cave. He smiled.

"I like this," he said. "Follow me." He shone the light toward the back of the cave and started to walk down a tunnel.

"We're entering the caves of Hypnos," he told her as they walked. "The river Lethe runs through here. You cannot drink the water from the river, no matter what. To do so causes you to forget everything. You will know nothing of your life, of what it is to be mortal. All you'll want is to meet the Judges and move on. It removes all sorrow, but also all joy." He paused, glancing back at her. "Do you understand?"

"Yes," she replied. "Don't drink the water."

"The cave will amplify your weariness," he continued. One more bend and they'd be able to stop before going too deep into the caves. "You'll be able to rest, but we will have to keep moving in the morning and find Kate. I believe she's in here." He looked back at Amber. "If you stop for too long, the urge to sleep will overtake you, and the urge to take a single sip of water will grow when you wake again. I hope we can find your friend before she's lost to the influence of the caves, or encounters the Ferryman that tends the river running through them."

They came around the bend and into a natural opening. Two cots sat against the walls. "We rest here," he told her.

She shrugged out of the pack, letting it fall with a thud to the floor, before collapsing on a bed.

"We should eat," he told her. "Do you have anything?"

"I've got some protein bars and dried fruit," she told him. Sitting back up, she dug through the pack.

He placed the flashlight on the floor, the beam pointing upward to illuminate as much of the room as he could. Amber held out a couple of things to him.

"Thank you," he said as he took the food. Moving over to the other bed, he looked at the food closer. Unsure what surrounded it, he went to bite into it.

Amber was in front of him, moving his hand away from his mouth. With a strange look on her face, she took it from his hand and tore it open. She pulled a bar out and handed it to him.

"What was that?"

"A wrapper," she replied. "They're used to keep the food fresh, and uncontaminated. Not very tasty though."

He bit into the bar and chewed. "I think I warned you that I would need to learn about your world more. Do you not hunt for your food? Grow it in fields?"

"We do. Well, some people do. Most of the rest of us go to stores and buy what we need. You've got people who farm the food, raise the animals for meat. Some people like to have small gardens where they can grow their own vegetables. Others like to hunt or fish. The rest of us, though, go to a store and buy our food that way."

Charon looked at the item in his hand, "Someone grew this?"

Amber laughed, "Not really. The raw ingredients were grown. Then a company buys those components and has it shipped to a factory where they're combined into the final product. Then it gets packaged, boxed up, and shipped to stores to be sold."

"Do you have your own garden?"

"No," she said as she curled her feet up under her. "There's room for a garden. I think Amanda had one at some point. But I don't have much of a green thumb."

He nodded, accepting her answer. They ate in silence for a few minutes.

"Amber, who is Heath?"

He heard her take a deep breath. "Heath is someone I was dating."

"You fought with him before summoning me. Why?"

"I'm not sure, really. He thinks I'm hiding things from him. But it's hard for me to explain everything about being your Guardian. I told him the basics, but he thinks you're a monster. He saw what was left of Bruce, doesn't think a man could do that to another. And he doesn't remember much from that night. Bruce beat him unconscious, so he never saw you or your boat. Only the mist. But it's hard for me to describe what it's like to guide the souls to you. He can't understand what that's like. And I won't let him be at the house on a full moon. I need time to prepare for the night. I can't just watch movies with him until midnight, dash outside, and come back."

"You fear him. I felt it. Why? Nothing I saw indicated he has raised a hand against you in anger."

"He's got this plan for our lives together. It's all mapped out for him. And he didn't ask me if I wanted any of it, just figured I would." Her voice rose slightly. "He wants me to sell my house, live what he calls a 'normal life', and let someone else be your Guardian. I don't know if I can do that."

"Do you love him?"

She didn't answer right away. When she did, her voice was soft. "No, not anymore. I think I did at one time. But he wants something out of life, something out of me, that I don't want to give up."

Conflicted, Charon stayed on his cot. Part of him wanted to comfort her, but he didn't know how. "Do you have questions about what happened with Amanda?" he asked, hoping to distract her mind.

"Where did she go?"

"She went on to meet the Judges. Most likely, they have allowed her to pass to Elysium now." He took a deep breath. "Please forgive me for taking you there. She was to stay there until a family member came through and forgave her. She was a good friend to me for many years, and I didn't want to see her spend decades beating herself up for the choice she made. I hoped that you could forgive her and allow her to move on, give her the peace she needed. It wasn't so far away that it would delay getting to Kate. If anything, it helped pinpoint her location more after I linked with you."

"You used me?" Amber demanded.

Charon drew breath but a deafening howl echoed through the cavern. "I didn't ask a question, Guardian!" Another howl answered the first. "Hellhounds … they're tracking us now. We have to leave." He darted to the center and picked up the flashlight. "Move!" he demanded.

He didn't wait for her to finish putting the pack on before he shoved the light into her hands. "Go that way," he pointed to the opening opposite of where they came in. "I'll catch up with you. Whatever you do, don't speak to anyone except Kate, if you find her. And don't drink anything you didn't bring in that pack of yours!" He pushed her forward. "Don't look back!"

Turning, he let his eyes adjust to the darkness. He'd put a staff in this room ages ago when he'd last been here with a Guardian. But where? The hounds bayed again, closer. They'd picked up their scent out at the base of the trail.

There! He climbed on one of the cots and reached into a small hole in the wall. His hands grasped the butt of the staff. Quickly, he pulled it free of the wall and moved back to the center of the room. He had enough time to center his body and get ready for the hounds to arrive.

Footsteps came closer. Padded feet on the cave floor. And…Charon cocked his head. Boots? A deep purple glow began to seep down the hallway, inching toward him.

Hades was coming.

He shifted the staff in his hands but kept his muscles at the ready. Amber needed time to get further into Hypno's depths and lost from His senses.

"I'm somewhat impressed, Charon." The god walked into the room, Cerberus at his side. "She got this far without making a mistake. I figured she'd be chatting your ear off when I released her."

"She's stronger than you think, Hades."

Leaning against the wall, the dark-haired man smiled at him. "Yes, she probably is. Which is all well and good. Because now she's without her Guardian. And navigating the caves without your help." He smiled, but the mirth didn't reach his eyes. "I don't appreciate what you did for Amanda, Charon. I wanted her to stay there, contemplate what she'd done, for a very long time. Long past when her niece died and refused to forgive her again. Amber's mother would've compounded her guilt. Instead, you managed to create a situation where Amber would forgive her, let her move on. You've taken away one of my amusements." His face changed, growing stone-cold. "So allow me to return the favor."

The staff began to vibrate in Charon's hands. The smooth, worn wood shifted into the wire wrapped hilt of a longsword. His sword. The blade, bathed in rivulets of crimson, stood out in the purple light. His hands shook. He swore never to hold this again, in anger or peace. Yet there it was, resting in his palms, feeling so much a part of him that it terrified him.

Charon held his stance as the god moved closer to him. "You think you're delaying me from chasing her down, don't you? That she's going to get away?" Cold hands cradled his face as Hades forced him to look him in the eye. "She doesn't know what you did yet. What you're capable of. What you did with that blade. Why you drive the boat on Styx." The grin came back. "Do you think she'd trust you to keep her safe if she knew? Or would she run from you, screaming, like all the rest?" He released his hold on Charon and stepped back. "You haven't heard the news, have you? I decided that the ferryman for the river Lethe had served his penance. Let him move on to be judged. There's a new man at that rudder. One that is still dying to get to know Amber *much* better."

His pulse quickened. "You put Bruce on that ferry," he breathed.

Hades retreated, spreading his arms wide. "And now I've delayed you long enough for her to get so turned around in the caves that it's a race. Will you get to her before Bruce does? Run along, Charon. You'd best find your Guardian before he does. Maybe you can convince her the blood you've shed was worth it."

Charon bolted down the hallway, Hades' laughter spurring him forward.

Chapter Thirteen

Heath leaned against the wall, trying to avoid eye contact with anyone else in the room. Why, he wasn't sure. Heidi had been right. The group was a good mix of people, most of them he'd known since high school. He still felt the odd man out, though.

"You know," Heidi told him as she approached, "the whole purpose of a mingle is to do that. Mingle. Leaning against a wall sorta defeats the purpose."

"I'm not much into small talk," he replied. "Besides, what do I say? This isn't exactly a big city. I'm betting most of them know about me and Amber. And that she's not Christian."

"Doesn't matter to most of them. Sure, you've got one or two that are a bit more traditional. Jessa and Kate have been here several times. Even with Kate's faith, they were accepted." She gave him a direct look. "Not every Christian's a Bible thumper. Most of us actually follow the teachings over being judgmental about things that are different."

"I suppose."

Heidi opened her mouth, and then stopped, looking past Heath. Turning his head, he followed her gaze. Sheriff Taylor stood just outside the doorway. She was moving toward him. Heath placed his empty cup on a table and followed.

"I don't understand," Heidi said to the sheriff as Heath approached. "Why would you need to talk with my children down at the station?"

"Amber Cross gave us copies of some emails that were sent to her and Kate just before and right after the attack. We've traced them back to an account registered to Caleb. We need to question him, find out what he knows."

"What's going on?" Heath asked

Heidi turned around, "They think Caleb's involved in the bomb on Kate's shop," she stammered out.

"Please, ma'am. We'd like to keep this low key if we can. Nobody's under arrest or anything. We simply want to talk with your son. If you like, you can schedule an interview with our detectives over coming down right now. But we do need to talk to Caleb. With you present, and a lawyer as well if you want to bring one." He paused, "But we need to do this soon."

"Heath, could you get in touch with Larry Dixon for me? Have him meet us at the sheriff's office?" She took a deep breath. "Fine, Sheriff. Let's do this now. I'll get the kids and meet you there."

Heath nodded and headed down the hall of the church at a sprint. Digging his cell out of his pocket, he found Larry's number and called it.

"Hello?"

"Larry, it's Heath. Heidi asked me to give you a call. Sheriff Taylor's wanting to question her kids about the bombing. She was hoping you could meet them down at the station, give her a hand." He said as he pushed open the door and ran into the parking lot toward his car.

"Larry's not in town right now," a woman's voice interrupted him. "I'll send one of his associates down there when I can find one."

Heath sighed, fumbling for his keys in his pocket. "Okay," he said. "I'll go down, see if I can be of any help." He hung up the phone and got into his car.

The drive to the sheriff's department offices took him past Amber's street. Without realizing it, he turned down the road and headed to her house.

The porch light illuminated the entry, but the rest of the house was dark. She wasn't back yet, from wherever it was she went to. The whole idea of getting Kate's soul back still rang hollow to him. She'd needed to get away after the bombing. He could understand that. Why invent the whole idea of some god and underworld out of mythology? That she still met with the monster that shredded her ex every month bothered Heath, too. She was hiding something. There was no other reason why she'd refuse to let him spend the night on the full moon. If she'd let him see what went on, maybe he'd be okay with it.

Sighing, he pulled away from the curb and headed to the sheriff's office. Heidi needed him right now. All he could do was hope that Amber would see reason when she got back from wherever she went. They could leave, travel the world, live anywhere they wanted to. She needed to realize their life could be so much better if it wasn't for that damn house.

Twenty minutes later, he followed the deputy through the maze of cubicles that made up the sheriff's department.

"Wait here," the officer told him, pointing to a small line of chairs against a wall. As Heath sank into one of the seats, the deputy disappeared through a door.

He looked around the office. Cubicle walls separated the different areas. He could see the top of a white board on the far wall, the words 'Cauldron Bombing' in large letters at the top. Curiosity got the better of him, and he rose from his seat. Looking around, he tried to gauge if he could make it back to the board without being stopped. As he took a step, the door opened back up.

"Got you cleared to watch, but they don't want you in the room. Follow me," the deputy told him.

The man led him to another door around the corner. Opening it up, he held and waited for Heath to enter.

The room was dark, with no chairs. A camera stood on a tripod, aimed at the glass that took up almost an entire wall. Sheriff Taylor nodded at him once, then turned back to the window.

Heath leaned against a wall and shoved his hands into his pockets. On the other side of the window, Heidi sat with both of her kids and a man in a suit. They were talking, but no sound filtered into the room.

The man in the suit stood and rapped against the glass. "Get ready to record," Taylor told the other officer in the room. He glanced at Heath, "Don't say a word. You're only here because Heidi wanted you to be." He opened the door and left.

A minute later, he walked into the room with Heidi and the rest. The deputy pushed a button on the camera.

"Just so you know, Heidi, we're recording now." The sheriff's voice was low, calm.

"That's fine. I understand," she said to him. She turned to Caleb and placed a hand on his. "Go ahead, Caleb. Tell the sheriff what you told me and Mr. Hoffman."

The boy took a deep breath. "I sent the emails. All of them."

Taylor leaned against the wall, "Okay, so who told you that there was going to be a problem?"

"That was me," Tamara said. Heidi put her other hand on her daughter's arm, reassuring her. The girl took a deep breath. "I didn't send the bomb or anything. It was someone else."

"Tell them everything, Tamara," Heidi encouraged her.

"A few weeks after we found out Dad had been killed, the school counselor set me up with a support group online. We were all supposed to be kids who had a parent die in Afghanistan. It was good to talk to other kids that understood." She took a deep breath. "I started to get messages from someone else, though. At first, they were really sympathetic. They said they understood and would help me in ways no one else could. They asked me about the rest of my family. When I told her about Aunt Jessa marrying Aunt Kate, she told me that it was their fault that my Dad was dead. That God was mad at me for having an aunt that was gay, and that Kate being Wiccan was wrong as well. She told me that Dad wouldn't be allowed in Heaven unless I chased them from my life." Tears started to flow down her cheeks. "I didn't want them to get hurt, but I was so scared. She said Dad was going to burn in Hell unless I told her where Kate's shop was. I thought I was helping my Dad. I didn't know she'd hurt Kate like that."

Heidi embraced Tamara, pulling her close as the girl cried.

"Tamara, do you have anything to help us? A name, address?" Taylor asked.

"Just her screen name. I didn't get anything else but that. But I told her about The Cauldron, about Aunt Kate and Amber. I'm the one that did this."

"No, Tamara. You're not. Someone else did this by taking advantage of you." Taylor pulled out a chair next to the girl and sat down. "You're not in trouble. But we need to see your computer, have your password for the chat room. Okay?"

The girl nodded. Taylor looked at the lawyer, who handed him a pad of paper and a pen. Pushing it to the girl, he asked, "Go ahead and write down your login information and the name of the chat room. We'll take a look. Heidi"—he looked at the woman as Tamara started to write— "can you bring her computer down here? We need our IT forensics team to take a look at the system itself to help track this person down."

Heath took a deep breath. Someone manipulated Heidi's kids, used their dad's death as a way to get to Kate and Amber. Anger boiled up inside him. He nodded once to the deputy, then left the room quietly.

He'd heard enough. He had some of his own investigating to do.

Chapter Fourteen

Amber ran, the light from the flashlight bouncing off from the cave walls with every step. Fear drove her. The howling of the dogs spurred her forward. Without thinking, she followed each twist and turn of the cavern. It wasn't until she faced a dead end that she stopped.

Putting her back to a wall, she slid down to the floor. *Breathe*, she chided herself. *Just breathe. Then think.* Concentrating on slowing her breathing, finding her center again, she let the last edges of panic ebb away.

Damn it, she thought. She wasn't mad at Charon. Not anymore. She'd been curious about what happened between Amanda and her mother since the day Larry showed up in their living room. She had the answers now. If anything, her issues with her mom went even deeper. How much did that woman pay Bruce to date her? A chill ran through her body. Given what she now knew, it was possible that her mother knew he'd tried to rape her. And still tried to push for them to get married.

She shoved the anger aside. It wasn't going to help her now. She turned off the flashlight and listened. The barking and growling had stopped. Charon had warned her not to drink or eat anything beyond what's in her pack, promised he'd find her. That didn't mean she had to make it easy for anyone or anything else to locate her. Time to be smart about where she was, over running blindly.

And she still had to find Kate.

Charon led her here, said Kate was here. Somewhere. The trick would be to find her before she was too far gone.

Slowly, she rose to her feet, trying to be as quiet as possible. Amber had to be quiet now, resourceful. Alert. Who knew when Charon would find her, or if he would. She did some quick calculations in her mind. Hades told her she had to be back home by the new moon. That gave her a week at most now. Better to plan on finding Kate and being back on Charon's boat within the next five days.

If he wasn't there, she wanted time to navigate the way back.

A wave of weariness washed over her. She was beyond tired. Charon's warning echoed in her head. Without him, she had no way of knowing where it would be safe to rest.

For a brief moment, she considered trying to find her way back to the area she'd run from. It was safe, and she needed to sleep. *No,* she thought, *I can't.* That's where whatever made that howling would go.

Taking a deep breath, she adjusted the pack to sit on her shoulders easier, then buckled the waist strap. She leaned against the wall, trying to determine which way she'd come. Darkness surrounded her. As her eyes adjusted, she could make out the faintest outline of the walls around her. She put a hand against one wall. It was damp.

She pulled her hand back and rubbed it against her jeans to dry it off. Tugging at the sleeve of her jacket, she covered her palm with some of the fabric. It wasn't perfect, but would offer some protection. If she couldn't drink the water, she wasn't so sure that having it seep in through her skin was a good idea, either.

With one hand against the wall, she started to move forward. Each time her hand found a new tunnel, she paused. Listening for any movement, she waited, holding her breath. Never moving again until she knew it was clear.

The sound of water drew her forward in the dark. The river flowed through the center of the cave system. It would serve to give her a sense of direction, at least. Follow the bank, keep it to one side of her, and she'd eventually find an exit. She hoped it worked that way, anyway.

The tunnel widened, opening up to a ledge. Some sort of dim light filtered through the other side, allowing her to make out the general layout. The cavern was enormous! The ceiling disappeared into the darkness above. Below, a ribbon of water cut through the floor. *Lethe*, she told herself. Each side of the cavern was dotted with outcroppings of rock. Some looked to have cave openings behind them. Others were nothing more than ledges of varying sizes.

Studying it even further, Amber started to make out the possibility of a path down. If she could leap or climb from each one. She needed more light, though. Squinting, she looked at the faint beam that pierced the far side. Given when she and Charon came down here, it was probably moonlight. If she could wait for morning, stay safe. It should give her enough light.

Something dark shifted on an outcropping nearest the opening. Amber retreated, but whatever was over there stopped. Keeping her movements as small and quiet as possible, she found a handhold and pulled herself up on the closest outcropping. No cave opened behind it, and there was only the one way up or down. Charon had a way to sense Kate. Hopefully, it worked on her as well. She undid the waist strap and lowered the pack off her back and onto the ground. Moving a zipper as slowly and as little as possible, she opened the pocket where she'd put the few bottles of water before she left. She removed one, closed the pack again, and sat on the ground. Easing back against the rough stone wall, she stretched her legs out in front of her as she drank the water. *Don't drink from the river,* she told herself with each sip. There wasn't much in her pack, she'd have to be careful with it.

Staying awake, that would be the challenge. The caves encouraged you to sleep, Charon said. And made the desire to drink even worse.

Kate needs you, Amber. So does Jessa. You've been through worse. She took a deep breath. If she laid down, it'd lower her profile. Less likely to be spotted from anyone below her. She stretched out, placing her head on the pack. Mentally, she began to recite every single song she could remember the lyrics to as her eyes focused on the sliver of moonlight. And prayed that Charon would find her before the exhaustion overtook her.

***

The Sandman looked at the two women, disgusted. The laughter had subsided, turned to a shrieking that was worse than fingernails on a chalkboard. "Shut up!" He roared at them. The two cowered, but their bodies still convulsed. He let out a heavy sigh. Maybe making them experience the pain of being tickled incessantly wasn't quite driving his point home.

Then again, Hades told him his job was to make them drink from Lethe, forget the pain they caused in life. Take that pain on himself. Some crap about learning what it felt like. Complete bullshit. He didn't care who he hurt in life. Why should he care in death?

Hades hadn't exactly kept his promises, either. Sold him a bunch of crap, that's what he'd done. Said this was an easy job, where he'd live in comfort and ease. Surrounded by creatures to do his every bidding. All he had to do was make sure the souls that came to this river forgot the bad things that'd happened to them in life.

Only this wasn't anything close to a palace. It was a cave. Dank, moldy, and cold. The creatures that served him? Most of the Oneiroi were barely recognizable as once being human. Their thin, skeletal bodies were covered with a sickly gray skin from the eons out of the sun. The way they moved, scurrying on all fours like some sort of dog, made him shudder.

But it was their faces, twisted into grimaces that were always turned to one side, that were the true thing of nightmares.

They were demonic, evil. And not at all pretty. And he'd always surrounded himself with pretty things. Nothing ugly. Not until now.

He shifted; the shredded skin on his back burned still. Charon's scythe had bit deep into his flesh. The wounds seeped constantly. Rivulets of pus and blood mixing with his own sweat constantly reminding him that he wasn't alive any more. That nothing around him was, either.

Wait, he thought. That wasn't true anymore. There was someone alive in here. He could feel the slow beating of their hearts. The steady rhythm of lungs breathing.

Two of them in the caves. His domain. One was a soul, though not quite dead. That one would be a challenge, but eventually would drink.

The other one...they were alive. Mortal. A malicious grin split his face. He'd play with them, make them think he'd help them. Only when they trusted him, would he make it clear they'd never return to the mortal plane.

One of the women whimpered again. He looked at the creature that hovered over the pair. "Phobetor," he said, "leave those for now. There's two others in Hypno's caverns. Summon your beasts, hunt them down, and bring them to me."

"Yes, Manases," the creature replied.

His eyes narrowed, "Don't ever call me that."

Phobetor straightened. "It's the name of the ferryman for Lethe. Bestowed upon you when Hades allowed your predecessor to move on to Elysium. It is a name with honor."

"I. Don't. Care." He spoke through a clenched jaw. "I am the Sandman. I bring sleep to those who need it."

Phobetor smiled, but his face was devoid of mirth. "You will learn soon enough that one does not defy Hades."

Before he could answer, the man left the room. Settling back into his chair, he turned to the cowering women. If the live one could be found, and restrained, he might actually let them drink the water. And forget everything he'd done to them.

Chapter Fifteen

Charon leaned with a thud against the wall, the sword still in his hands. The tip scraped against the floor. His hands around the hilt felt at home. Centuries had come and gone since he'd wrapped his fingers around the weapon, but the muscles had not forgotten.

Of course they hadn't. Because Hades hadn't let him drink from Lethe. He would never be allowed to forget.

Think, he chided himself. Amber had run off, at his insistence, but the caves were extensive. He sensed her, the same as he did Kate, but couldn't pinpoint where she was. Just that she was in here. And alive.

The more he ran about, the more lost he'd become. Without any real clue on how to find either of the women, he was as lost as they were. The only two advantages he had were knowing how to get to the river, and how to get out of the caves.

Well, that and being immune to the cave's effects. He couldn't forget until Hades allowed it, no matter how much of the river he drank. If Manases even allowed him to.

He pushed himself away from the wall. That could be it. Head to the ferryman's home, see if any of the Oneiroi would help him. His fingers tightened around the hilt.

If Manases—Bruce—tried to block him, Charon would find out just how much fighting skill he still had.

He started off, allowing his senses to guide him. It was something Hades had instilled in all His ferrymen—the ability to find the others. Not out of any sense of companionship or loyalty to each other. More so they didn't try to catch each other unawares. Centuries before, there were two siblings. Conjoined twins in life, separate souls in the underworld. One was sent before the Judges, allowed to enter Elysium. The other became the Ferryman for Archeron, the River of Woe. Despite being conjoined, they were extremely different people. The ferryman became enraged, unable to believe their brother had been given something they hadn't. He found a way to kill that which was already dead and began to slaughter the other ferryman, hoping that Hades would be forced to bring his brother back to him.

It wasn't pretty.

When the bloodbath was over, Hades changed each of them. Made them aware of each other at all times, so no river was ever left unattended.

At least, in theory. Charon had more leeway than most. But he'd been at his post for the longest. And had no problem obeying commands.

He turned another corner, then came to a dead stop. A solid rock wall blocked the tunnel, one he knew should've been there. *"Filius canis,"* he muttered, the curse rolling off of his tongue. The dead language he'd been taught as a youth came back to him far too easily.

"Manases," he yelled, "I don't know what game you're playing. But I will find you. You cannot block all of the passages to your lair. Hades would not allow that."

"This is my realm, brother." Sarcasm dripped from the voice that echoed through the chamber. "Not yours. Go back to Styx. You do not dictate *anything* here."

Charon took a step back, scanning the wall in front of him. "Both of us serve at the will of Hades, brother. Do not make this difficult on yourself." He moved forward, leveling his sword out in front of him. As the tip touched the rock face, the illusion melted away.

Lowering the blade, he moved down the tunnel. A series of steps, cut out of the rock, spiraled down into the hidden valley below. The river ran through the center, a constantly moving inky darkness. To his left, the home of the ferryman stood. Carved out of the rock itself, the fires inside illuminated the structure. Charon paused. He'd been here several times. The ferryman before Bruce had been his friend for many, many years. Always had he been welcoming to the souls, taking his task seriously. The bright glow emanating from the house was too much. It gave the impression of fear, hatred, dread. Any soul coming here to forget wouldn't be treated with compassion.

"That's not our job, Manases. We're not here to be nice."

The man's jaw tightened in the dim light. "Don't call me that. I prefer Sandman."

"It is the name Hades gave you, the name of the office. You cannot change it based on your own desires."

He stepped closer, "It's not my name. My name was Bruce. Until you decided to murder me to protect some whore!"

Charon leveled his gaze, satisfaction washing over him as Bruce noticeably withered under his scrutiny. "Your own actions caused your death. The Guardian gave you instructions. Ones that would have allowed you to live if you'd followed them. Your own arrogance led to your death. Though"—he moved forward a single step, closing the small gap between them— "I will admit that I took some pleasure in handing out your doom. I saw what you did to my Guardian. What her mother paid you to do to her. And I will gladly add a few more cuts to your back if you do not take me to her and Kate. Right now."

Bruce swallowed, his face going pale. *Good,* Charon thought. *He remembers what my blade felt like.*

"I..." he stammered. "I don't know who you're talking about. There's no one here but me and those blasted nightmares Hades left to keep me company."

Charon grabbed hold of the front of the other man's shirt and lifted him closer to his face. "You were a horrible liar in life, and even worse in death. I can feel them. Both of them. And the two other women you have in chains in your house. The two you're torturing until they do your bidding. That is not what your job is about, *Manases*. And my Guardian and her friend do not belong here. Not yet. You will take me to them. All of them. You're going to set the two free and have them drink from Lethe so they can move on. Amber, Kate, and I are going to leave the caves. And you'd better pray that Hades doesn't come here to ask why." The last was a gamble on his part. Hades had orchestrated this whole thing, and Charon knew it. He hoped that Bruce was too new to his job to realize that.

Nodding, he replied. "Fine. Put me down and we'll go inside the house."

Charon dropped him back to the ground and shoved him as he let go. Extending his sword so it was more than visible, he motioned to the house. "You first," he said.

Straitening his tunic, Bruce started to walk toward the cave. Charon fell into step behind him, his thumb rubbing the leather wrapped hilt. He didn't trust him. Until they were free of the caves, he was going to be ready for trouble.

The first room held Bruce's prisoners. Charon leaned against a wall, watching as the chains were removed and Bruce moved a round tile in the floor. The waters of Lethe bubbled up through the opening, and both women scrambled to drink. As the effects began to work, their faces changed. All the problems and worries that'd plagued them in life, the pain and losses, fell from their shoulders as small drops of mercury. The beads moved steadily over to Bruce, climbing up his shoes and disappearing under the leg of his pants.

The ferryman changed, as well. Lines broke open on his hands and neck. The wounds began to seep. "Thank you," one of the women said. Turning his head back to the sound, he saw the two souls turn to mist and float out of the room.

"Happy?" Bruce snapped at him.

"No," Charon replied. "Take me to Amber. Now."

Bruce glared at him, not even bothering to hide his hatred. "This way," he said as he headed to a staircase hidden in an alcove. "I haven't hurt her."

"You wanted to, though. You still do."

"And you want to be some fuckin' knight in shining armor, rescuing her from evil." Bruce retorted.

"She is my Guardian, and I am hers. That's all."

Bruce stopped next to a door. He snorted, "If that's what you want to tell yourself. I can read you as easily as you read me. You'd ride her the minute she showed any interest."

"Manases, you will learn there is more to living than sex. There's more to death than revenge. But you have to learn that on your own. I did." He pushed open the door.

Amber was inside, laying on a cot. Her chest rising in slow, even breaths. On another cot lay a second woman. Her back was to him. She had dark, curly hair. His senses told him it was Kate. "Stand over there," Charon commanded Bruce, pointing to a spot on the far side of the room. He waited for him to move before sitting on the edge of the cot. Raising his head, he kept his attention on Bruce as he gently shook her shoulder. "Guardian? Wake up. We need to find Kate."

She stirred, but didn't wake up. "What did you give her," he demanded.

"Nothing, really. I mean, it's possible that Phobetor had to give her some water to quiet her down, but that's all." The smirk on his face told Charon it was more than a little water.

He glanced at Amber. "Please don't hate me for this," he muttered. Reaching his hand out, he placed the palm on the top of her head.

And forced her to remember the days leading up to her trip into the Underworld.

Her eyes flew open, and she stared at him. Pain and fear filled her face. He moved his hand away from her head. "I'm sorry," he told her. "But you wouldn't wake up. That was the only way."

She swallowed, nodding once. He moved so she could sit up. "Look beside you," he commanded. "Is that who you seek?" Bruce stood out of her line of sight, and Charon hoped she wouldn't see him.

Amber twisted her body, glancing at the other cot. Nodding vigorously, she looked back at him.

"You don't have much time, Guardian. Do not waste it on revenge. I will step outside. Be mindful of the geas Hades put on you." He rose from the cot. He watched Amber to make sure her attention wasn't on him, then pulled Bruce out of the room with him.

Once they were both out, he shut the door and leaned against the frame. No one was going in that room until Amber came out.

***

*F*ive *minutes, Amber. That's all the time you have.* Not wanting to waste any of it, she moved to the cot. *Wake her up first,* she thought, *then talk.* A wave of nausea crashed over her when she tried to stand up. She blinked, shaking her head from side to side, and rode it out. Standing, she shoved the pain aside. *You've got a job to do, woman. So do it.*

She made her way over to Kate. Her breathing was strong and steady. Good. No visible cuts or bruises. Even better. Easing herself to the floor, she made sure her legs were comfortable. She had to focus on her friend, not pins and needles in her legs.

Reaching out, she started to shake Kate's shoulder. Her friend moved a little, but didn't wake up. Biting her lip to keep from talking, she tried to think of ways to rouse her. She couldn't do what Charon had done to her. And she didn't want to, either. She understood why he did it, didn't blame him. But having those memories forced back into her head while she slept had probably caused the nausea. The shock and pain had set every nerve in her body on fire.

Her eyes flew open. That was it! Taking a deep breath, she moved Kate's hand. Opening it up, she placed her thumb and forefinger on the skin between hers and started to dig her fingernails into the flesh.

Kate's body jerked. Amber grabbed her wrist and kept digging. Holding tight, she kept at it as Kate thrashed even more. Finally, a small cry came from her mouth. Amber released her hold and grabbed her shoulders, pulling her upright.

She looked into her friend's blue eyes, seeing the confusion. "Kate, listen to me. I can't talk long. Do you remember the explosion?"

Looking away, Kate nodded. "Yes, I think so. There was a box waiting outside The Cauldron."

"That's right."

"I went to open it," she paused. Her eyes flew open wide. "There was something inside….it exploded….I woke up and something wasn't right."

"You're in the Underworld, Kate. You're still alive, but in a coma. The bomb forced your soul from your body."

She shook her head in disbelief. "Who, Amber? Who would do that?"

"I don't know. But Sheriff Taylor's trying to find out. He might know by now. That's not important right now. You and I have to be back on Charon's boat before dark. We have to be back at my house, back on the mortal plane, before the new moon. Or Hades will make us stay here."

Kate nodded, swallowing hard. "Just tell me where to go, what to do."

"Don't talk. Not until we get back to my house. If Charon says we're in a safe place, and asks you a question, then you must answer it fully. Otherwise, we stay silent. No matter what."

"If we don't?"

Amber took a deep breath. "You don't want to know."

Something landed against the wall closest to the door. Turning her head to the noise, she saw the wall shudder from the impact. She was running out of time.

Rising from the floor, she reached a hand out and helped Kate rise. "Come on. Let's get you home to Jessa." She led her to the door, relief filling her. She'd found Kate in time, convinced her to come back. The hard part was over.

Swinging open the door, she stopped in her tracks. Charon stood there, a sword in his hand. The tip rested against Bruce's throat. The hope she'd felt moments ago faded, replaced by anger and fear.

"Is everything done, Guardian?" Charon asked her.

She moved to Charon's side, pulling Kate with her. Bruce glared at her. What was he doing here? Nodding at Charon, she kept her eyes on her ex. She didn't trust him in life. No way would that change now.

"Good." Charon turned his attention back to his prisoner. "Manases, *brother*, we're leaving now. You will not have us followed. You will stay here and do your job. Correctly. Hades will be watching you. If He commands it, I'll be more than happy to come back and remind you what your duties really are." He turned his head slightly, "Guardian, follow this hallway to a staircase. Take it down and then head out to the river's edge. I'll be right behind you."

She nodded and grabbed Kate's hand. They started to move quickly down the hallway. Charon wasn't done with Bruce. But whatever else he wanted to say or do, he didn't want her to witness it.

***

They made it down the staircase and found the edge of the river. When they stopped, Kate opened her mouth. Amber held up her hand to stop her. She went to grab for the pad of paper, realizing her pack wasn't with her. Last time she'd seen it, it was sitting on the ledge next to her.

Damn it, she thought. Thinking fast, she knelt down and scribbled the words, 'don't talk', in the thin layer of dirt.

Kate nodded in understanding. Without her pack, or the paper and pencil she'd been given by Amanda, this was going to make things difficult. At least until they got home.

A figure moved toward them and Amber straightened. The hilt of a sword moved with his step.

"Are you both all right, Guardian?" Charon asked as he approached.

She nodded.

He looked at Kate. "I am Charon. I will get you both home. But you must listen to me. If I say run, then run. If I say stop, then stop. Time is running out, and it's not over yet. Do you understand?"

Amber looked over at her friend and saw her nod.

"Good. We head that way," he pointed toward the sliver of light in the distance. "There's a place to cross the river safely. Manases told me about it just now. Your feet will likely get wet, but the river won't affect you unless you drink from it. If we move fast enough, we will be on my boat before dark." He turned back to Amber, his face puzzled. "Guardian, where's your pack?"

She held up her hands and shrugged.

"We're still in a safe place. Again, where is your pack?"

"I don't know." She kept her voice low. "I took it off and sat down. I was waiting for dawn, figuring more light would come through. I think I was over that way," she pointed up the side of the wall. "Next thing I knew, you were waking me up."

"*Faex*!" Charon exclaimed.

Amber looked at him, puzzled.

"Sorry," he replied. "I prefer to swear in Latin. Few understand it that way." He took a deep breath. "Either it's still there, or Manases has it. And I'd rather check the ledge. He's lazy. I doubt he would've retrieved either of you by himself. And the Oneiroi wouldn't have bothered with the pack. There's more stairs around here, we just need to look for the right one."

Amber scanned the tall walls surrounding them. She could barely make out what Charon was talking about. Every hundred feet or so, a darker ribbon spiraled upward.

Something tugged at her leg. Looking down, Kate had knelt and written, "Why do we need it?" in the dirt.

"The pack has the bag of coins that belongs to the Guardian. Without them, you won't be able to pay my fee when we get back to the waystation. You'll be trapped here. Forever." Straightening his shoulders, he continued. "We move, now. Time is against us as it is."

Taking a few deep breaths, she found her center. She started to walk toward the wall, her gaze trying to find some sort of landmark to pinpoint the ledge she'd been on.

Her mind filled with questions. About how Bruce ended up here, why Charon called him Manases. But she knew better than to ask. If she remembered, and it was possible, she'd ask when they got back home. *Charon might not be able to answer, though.*

None of that would matter, though, if they didn't find the pack.

Chapter Sixteen

"**G**uardian! Up here!" Charon called down to Amber.

She looked at Kate, motioning her to stay put. No reason for her to finish the climb if the pack was found.

Turning, she glanced up at the ledge. Charon stood there, her pack in hand. He tossed it at her, "Check it," he commanded. "Make sure everything's there."

Catching the bag, she knelt on the ground. Her hands went to the zipper on the side pocket where she'd placed the pouch. Pulling it open, she found the bag. She freed it from the pack and tossed it lightly in her hand. The sound of coins jingling inside flooded her with relief.

"Open it, Guardian. Make sure the contents are correct." He climbed down from the ledge and stood next to her.

She untied the leather drawstring and shook a few coins out. The gold glittered in the dim light. She held her hand up to Charon, to show him.

His hand closed around hers. The warmth surprised her. She wasn't sure why, but it was unexpected. Both the warmth of his skin and the touch itself. "Put it away now, Guardian. Keep it safe. You will need that soon enough."

Nodding, she poured the coins back into the bag. Securing the string, she placed it back into the pack and zipped the pocket shut. She stood and donned it, making sure it rested easily on her shoulders before securing the waist strap.

Glancing up at Charon, she paused. His face was as impassive as always, but something different was there. It faded as he stepped back from her. "Go," he said, his voice quiet.

Amber started to make her way back down the stairs. Kate looked up at her, a question on her face. Amber patted the padded straps to indicate all was good. He friend smiled, then began the descent.

Charon kept them at a quick pace, following the banks of Lethe. The light grew brighter as dawn approached. Amber did the math as they marched. It didn't help that she had no idea exactly how time passed here vs. at home, but she thought today was the last day before the new moon. Which meant they had to get on Charon's ferry and back to her home before the sun rose.

No wonder he was pushing them so hard.

That, and she knew she was combating the effects of the cave system itself. Her feet took more effort to lift with every step. The pack on her back got heavier. All she wanted to do was sit and rest.

She trudged on, concentrating on the ground in front of her. The marrow in her bones began to scream for rest. Yet, somehow, she found the energy to take another step.

And ran smack into Charon's back.

He turned, concern on his face. His hands rested on her arms, steadying her. It was all she could do to stand.

A fresh wave of exhaustion swept over her. Her eyes closed and she leaned forward, her head resting on his chest. She was safe with him. Surely she could sleep for a little bit. An hour should be enough.

"Amber, you have to fight this."

She didn't know whose voice was whispering in her ear. She didn't care. Sleep was overtaking her, surrounding her like a thick quilt on a cold, snowy night.

"Amber, think of Kate. She's relying on you to get her out of here. You promised to find her, bring her home. Fight this!"

Somewhere, deep in her soul, a light ignited. As it spread through her body, the weariness lifted. Opening her eyes, she found Charon staring down at her. "Are you better now, Guardian?"

She nodded her head. He pulled away, stepping back as he released her. "Kate, stay close. This area is dangerous. We cross over there," he pointed into the distance. "Then head up to the exit. Hypnos doesn't like to let souls go, and will work hard to make you sleep. Fight it. I can't carry you both."

Amber waited for Kate to come up next to her, then linked arms with her. Looking at her friend, she nodded once. They'd get through this together. She knew that now.

Charon led them to the banks. A series of rocks rose from the water, marking a path to cross. The water rushed around them, the force splashing up to cover the tops.

"Guardian, you will go first. I'll follow. Kate, you're last. Take your time, be sure of your steps." He held out his hand and grasped her wrist. Then did the same for Kate with his other hand. "We move in step with each other. Once you're on the other side, let go. I should be able to keep either of you from falling if you slip."

Carefully, Amber moved forward and stepped onto the first rock. They were smooth and flat, but barely large enough for one of her feet, let alone both. This would be harder than she thought. She'd not be able to stand on one at a time.

Stepping forward, she started to make her way across the stones. She could see the exit now. Up a steep incline, the bright light beckoned. The urge to run to the light, be out of the caves, started to grow inside her. *One step at a time,* she chanted in her mind. *Think of it as your reward. Everyone gets across the river safely first.*

With those thoughts running through her head, she worked her way across the stones. Charon's hand stayed steady around her wrist, moving with her. The water splashed up, soaking her shoes and socks. Ignoring the squishy feeling, she took the final steps onto the bank and let go of Charon's hand. Turning around, she waited for them to finish the crossing.

Kate's jaw was clenched, and her eyes were wide with fear. Charon had turned around to face her, taking both of her hands into his. Amber couldn't hear what he was saying to her, but the fear left Kate's face. He started to walk backwards, leading her with every step.

She'd have to ask Kate about that, later. When this was all over, and they were home. When she was awake from the coma, and out of the hospital.

Something told her they'd be drinking a lot of wine that night.

"Let's go," Charon said. Amber linked arms with Kate one more time and followed him up the steep incline.

The warm sunlight welcomed her as they emerged from the caves. The final edges of exhaustion faded away. Taking a moment, she reveled in the sense of freedom. She shielded her eyes and looked up, hoping to gauge the time.

The ball of light danced in erratic patterns across the sky.

"Hades!" Charon shouted into the valley below them. "Keep to your word!"

The scenery shifted. The brown turned to black glass as the obsidian dock materialized before them. Amber felt Kate's hand grab at her arm. Reaching over, she pulled her friend close.

The boat rocked gently alongside the dock, beckoning them. She looked at Charon. It was too easy. Would Hades really let them leave now, without a fight?

"Stay alert. No matter what, get her on the ferry. Once you're there, He can't stop you. And he can't kill me. I'm already dead."

Giving Kate a reassuring squeeze, she led her friend toward the dock. Her gaze stayed on the path in front of them.

"Leaving so soon, Amber?" Hades' voice came from her left. She didn't turn her head or respond, just kept walking with Kate.

Cerberus appeared in front of them, blocking the final ten feet to the boat. Each head bobbed lightly, watching them intently.

"She has fulfilled what she came to do, Hades." Charon spoke from behind her. "Do not dishonor yourself by reneging on your agreement."

Out of the corner of her eye, she saw a figure move. "But she didn't, Charon. She spoke, once, and asked you a question. That wasn't part of the deal. She wasn't supposed to ask anything. Just answer."

Amber felt Kate's body shivering. Her skin was turning cold. Alarmed, she glanced back at Charon.

"Keep walking," he instructed.

She bit her lip, and started to move toward Cerberus.

"But that's not what you said. You told her, 'With him, you can't start the conversation'. She didn't. I started it."

"I also stated she had to stay with you at all times!" Hades retorted.

The massive dog shifted and stood up, its' heads watching the two of them intently.

"But at no time did you say I couldn't send her away. Your exact terms were, 'you keep Charon with you at all times'. Do you really think I ever left her? I am her Guardian, as much as she is mine. I *always* knew where she was. I always will."

Swallowing her fear, Amber continued to walk toward the boat. They were close enough to reach out and touch Cerberus now. Her mind worked overtime, trying to find a way for them to move around the creature. Obsidian pillars sat to each side. There was no room between the heads and them to skirt around.

"Cerberus! Heel!" The dog's heads shifted at the call of their master and it loped off.

Unable to relax enough to celebrate, Amber kept leading Kate forward. They stepped onto the shallow deck. She eased her friend to a seat before taking one herself. Only then did she look back to the shore.

Hades said something to Charon, a look of spiteful vengeance on his face. Charon's own face darkened, the jawline clenching. He didn't reply, though. Instead, he turned and sprinted down the dock. His hands grabbed the mooring rope, undid the knot, and tossed it into the bow as he jumped down into the craft. With a smooth, practiced movement, his hands grasped the pole resting in the stern and began to move the boat forward.

"Hold her close, Guardian," he instructed her. "Your geas are gone, and she needs to hear your voice. Her soul is dying. The colder she gets, the smaller the chance for it to rejoin her body when we arrive."

Amber unclipped the strap to her pack and slid it off. Digging into the main section, she pulled out the jacket she'd thrown in at the last minute. She threw it over Kate's shoulders before grabbing her hands. "Stay with me," she told her as she tried frantically to warm her fingers. "You're safe now. We're taking you back home, back to Jessa."

The boat jerked forward as she continued to plead with Kate to keep fighting.

Chapter Seventeen

"Get ready."

Amber looked ahead. The mist cleared off the water's surface as the dock came into view. Her dock. "Kate, we're home. Just one more thing and you can go back to Jessa."

Kate raised her head. The meager light of the moon offered little illumination, but Amber could see the pale, translucent quality to her skin.

"When we get to the dock," she spoke quickly, urgently, "I'm going to help you up onto it. Think of Jessa, the shop, everything you hold dear. You'll find the thread to follow back to your body. I can't help you with that. It has to come from you. You have to want it." She looked over her shoulder at Charon. "Was that everything?"

"Yes," he replied.

Kate had steadily declined during the trip on Styx. As Amber talked to her and tried to keep her warm, Charon gave her instructions. The one thing missing from the book was what happened when she got her back home.

They came alongside the dock. Amber watched as Charon threw a rope around a pylon. She stood up and pulled Kate with her. Turning her around, she picked her up and raised her toward the platform. "Come on, Kate," she pleaded. "Fight for this. Fight for your life."

A scream ripped from Kate's body and she clawed her way forward. Amber continued to push her forward as she crawled. She collapsed, breathing heavily. Placing a hand on a pylon, Amber got out of the boat and went to her side. Kate raised her head, looking at her. The color was coming back to her skin. "Thank you," she whispered. Her body jerked violently, the back arching upward, before dissipating into a cloud of silver dust.

"Kate?" Amber whispered.

"She's heading back to her body, Guardian. You were successful."

She turned to Charon, surprised to see he stood on the dock. He'd never gotten out of his boat at the waystation before. Her pack was in his hand. "What's wrong?"

"You are still in danger, Guardian. Hades granted me a boon. I can remain until the half moon, no longer. Until you know who hurt Kate, you are not safe."

Stunned, she sat there, unsure what to say.

He looked at her, a slight smile on his face. "Dawn is coming. We may want to be inside before then."

Amber came to her senses and rose. "Yeah, that makes sense. Um, follow me." She held out her hand. "I can take the pack."

He looked at her and frowned. "Do you not trust me with it, Guardian?"

She smiled. "I do. But my house keys are in it. I need those to unlock the door."

Charon managed to look a little sheepish as he handed her the pack. "I apologize."

Taking the pack, she fished out the key ring and started to walk across the yard to the back door.

After walking in the house, she typed in the code for the alarm. Dropping the pack onto a bench, she flipped on a light switch. "Living room's down the hall and on the left. Go ahead and make yourself comfortable. I'm going to feed Minerva and make some coffee."

She strode into the kitchen, her hand turning on the light switch as she entered. "Minerva," she called out. "I'm home!" Opening the pantry, she found the cat's favorite food. She popped the lid and knelt down, shaking the contents into the bowl.

The calico came running into the kitchen, making a beeline for the food. Laughing, Amber reached out and stroked her long fur. "I know Larry fed you, Minerva. No use pretending you're starving."

The cat ignored her and kept eating.

She straightened up and tossed the can into the trash bin. Spying her cell phone on the charger, she grabbed it. Ignoring all the notifications, she sent a quick text to Larry. It was late, but she knew he'd see it in the morning. Shoving the phone in her pocket, she started to brew a couple of cups of coffee.

She carried the two steaming mugs toward the living room. "I hope black's okay," she called out. "I don't know how you like your coffee."

The room was dark. "Why are you sitting in the dark?" She asked him as she flipped the wall switch with her elbow.

Charon jumped up from the chair, his hand going to the sword leaning against the arm. "What did you do?" he asked her.

Handing over a mug, she said, "I turned on the lights. The wall switch over there"— she pointed to the doorway she'd just come through— "turns on the electricity to the lights."

He lowered himself back into the chair. Amber watched him closely as she settled herself onto the couch. His entire body was on alert. His gaze moved about the room, trying to take it all in.

"Charon, how long has it been since you were on the mortal plane?" She sipped her coffee, watching him.

"What year is it?"

"2018."

He took a drink from the mug. A look of pure enjoyment crossed his face. "It's been 920 years since I died. This world has changed more than I could imagine."

Her mind reeled from what he said. Almost a thousand years? There wasn't anything in the house that was even half that age.

"Why was Bruce in the caves? And why did you call him Manases and brother?"

Charon sipped from his mug again. "That is his name now. He is the ferryman for Lethe, the one who is to remove all painful memories and take on that burden. The name reflects the position. As he is also a ferryman, he is my brother. Even if I do not care for the relation." He took a breath and looked away from her. "Each river has a ferryman. Each one is put into the position by Hades, because we did something in our life that prevents us from going before the Judges. Only when we've redeemed ourselves to Hades' satisfaction, met all of his criteria, are we released. There must also be another soul coming in to replace us. The rivers cannot be left without a ferryman."

"So, Charon's not your name but your job title?"

He nodded. "I suppose. I have worn it for over nine hundred years. It is as much my name as my title now."

"Can I ask a personal question?"

"You are my Guardian, and I am yours. There should be no secrets between us."

She placed her mug on the coffee table and looked back at him. "Who were you, before you became Charon? And what did you do that made Hades give you the job?"

Pain and regret danced across his face. "I was the illegitimate son of a Count. I couldn't inherit, but he claimed me at least. Gave me more than a little bit of education, allowed me to be squired to a knight in his service. Thought I could make the Church my home, so he sent me to a monastery. I was twenty, but because I was a bastard, no family would consider me for their daughters. Being attached to a Holy Order, even as a soldier, was my best option. After a few years, the priests started preaching about the great Crusade, how we were God's own warriors. I listened to their sermons, grew to hate the infidels who had taken over Jerusalem. By the time our company got there, the zeal was absolute. Anyone that wasn't Christian, that was the smallest difference from what they said was holy, needed to die. I didn't care. I was going to do God's Will and cleanse the Holy City."

His voice dropped low. Placing the sword across the arms of the chair so it rested in front of him, his hands caressed the blade. The gesture made Amber's blood run cold.

"We got there in July. The weather was hot, oppressively so. My padding was soaked with sweat before I finished putting my armor on. But I didn't care. I could see the gates of Jerusalem. I had to do as the priests told me. I had to reclaim it for God and all of Christendom.

"The fighting lasted for hours before we finally breached the walls. I was among the first men to enter the city. By then, I was no longer myself. Everyone I saw that wasn't the same as me, wasn't a Crusader, needed to die. Many did, with this blade here. In my rage, I struck out at anyone that moved. Then I heard it."

"Heard what?" Amber asked, her voice hushed.

"The cry of a child cut short. The veil lifted from my sight and I saw this," he held the sword upright. "The sword given to me by my father. The one I swore would not dishonor his name. I saw it driven through a woman with a babe held close to her chest. I'd killed them both without thought." He lowered the weapon, resting it across the arms of his chair again.

"Minutes later, I was dead. I don't know who killed me. It could've been the husband of the family I'd just murdered in cold blood. It could've been a fellow Crusader, lost to the same battle fever I was. It doesn't matter. Hades locked me away for a time, with nothing but the screams of those I slaughtered for company. When He came to me, offered to give me a path to redemption, I agreed. And so, I became Charon. I became the judge, jury, and executioner I'd been in life. And I will not be released from the task until I fully understand my mistake."

"After all this time, Hades still doesn't think you've learned that murder is wrong?"

"It's not about the killing I did. It's why I did it." He leaned back in the chair. "I followed the priests blindly, believed every word they said. I didn't think about what was right or wrong. If they weren't the same as me, they were wrong. I judged them based on the color of their skin, the god the worshipped. Not on their character. I brought dishonor to my father, and this sword. It's good that I couldn't inherit his title. I wasn't worthy."

She sat back, trying to comprehend what he'd told her. He'd spent nine hundred years trying to atone for something. Something that still happened in the world now. A yawn escaped her. Despite the coffee, her body was unwilling to stay awake much longer.

"I'm going to head to bed," she told him. "Even if Kate wakes up before dawn, they'll notify Jessa first. I won't know for hours. Would you like me to show you where the spare room is?"

"No," he replied. His gaze still rested on the blade in his lap. "I will stay down here, if I sleep at all. I need to adjust to your world a bit."

She nodded and rose from the couch. With luck, her brain would be able to understand everything he told her in the morning. Pausing as she passed his chair, she asked, "What was your name? Before you became Charon?"

"William," he replied. "William Jordan of Toulouse."

Leaving him to his thoughts, she went up to her room. She collapsed on her bed, not bothering to remove her boots, and fell into a dreamless sleep.

Chapter Eighteen
New Moon

Something vibrated against her hip, rousing her from the dreamless sleep. She rolled over and looked at a clock. It was 9:30 am. She was in her room. Minerva was curled up at the foot of her bed.

Remembering the phone she'd left in her pocket, she pulled it out. One text, from Jessa. *THANK YOU!!!!*

Kate was awake from the coma.

Relief flooded through her. She was stiff, sore, and still felt tired. But it'd worked. Kate's soul had made it back to her body in time.

Sitting up, she remembered Charon was downstairs. She'd get down there soon enough. Right now, she needed a shower. Clean clothes.

Twenty minutes later, she headed down to the main level. "Are you awake?" she called out as she jogged down the staircase.

"Yes," Charon replied.

Turning the corner, she entered the living room. He was still sitting in the chair. "Kate's going to be fine. I got a message from Jessa." She told him as she walked in. "Why don't you go upstairs, take a shower?" she suggested. "I'll get started on some breakfast."

He rose, leaning the sword against the fireplace. "What's a shower?"

She smiled. "Head up the stairs, open the center door on the left side of the hallway. There's a bathtub. Turn the knobs to add hot or cold water. I'll teach you about the shower later." She looked him over. "We'll do some shopping later, get you some new clothes. I know you won't be here long, but you can't wear the same clothes for two weeks."

He didn't say a word. Simply nodded and headed up to follow her directions.

Amber went into the kitchen. Minerva darted out of a doorway, rubbing against her legs. Laughing, she fed the cat first. Then she started to get breakfast ready.

She wasn't sure what he'd like to eat. There wasn't much in the fridge, anyway. Enough to make scrambled eggs. Digging in the freezer, she found some brown and serve sausages. That'd have to do.

Footsteps echoed in the hallway, heading her way. "It's almost done," she called out as she turned the sausage one more time.

"I missed you, too." Heath said, his voice quiet.

She turned, surprised. He leaned against the archway leading to the dining room. For a moment, she wondered how he got in. Then remembered she didn't lock the house or turn on the alarm after they got back. "Hi," she replied. "I, um, didn't expect you."

He walked over and sat in one of the chairs at the island. "I heard Kate was awake. Figured that meant you were back."

She went back to cooking, trying to think of something to say. Things had changed between them. *Just tell him,* she admonished herself. "Heath," she took a deep breath, "I did a lot of thinking on this trip…"

"So did I. While you were gone. I mean, I understand why you got mad and all. It's all of this baggage that came with your house. It's weighing you down … dragging us with it. If you'd just consider selling, we could go back to how things were."

Amber turned, crossing her arms. She looked straight at him, determined for him to hear her. "It's not going to happen. I love this house. I love my job. I'm not giving those up for anyone."

"Guardian, I noticed there was a library upstairs. Do you mind," Charon stopped as he entered the kitchen. He looked at her and then Heath. "My apologies. I didn't know you had a guest."

She saw Heath's face darken and knew what he was thinking. A strange man, bare chested and with wet hair, in her house. This wasn't going to end well, no matter what she said. The temperature in the room was getting colder by the second.

"This is Heath. Heath, this is William Jordan. He's a friend of mine. From France." Hopefully, that would explain the slight accent. And Heath would believe her.

***

He went to extend his hand in greeting to Heath when he noticed neither one of them was moving. Time stopped.

"Well, this is…unexpected." Hades said.

Looking toward the sound, he watched the god enter the room. "Of all the scenarios I played out over time in my head that you might be released from my service, I never expected it to look like this. You have a jilted lover," He placed a hand on Heath's shoulder. "Or, rather, one about to be. I don't think he quite understands that yet. Though you walking into the room like this certainly has him convinced you and Amber slept together last night." He moved closer to Amber. "And then there's the woman who freed you. Of course, neither of you knew it took someone using your real name and calling you 'friend' to do that."

Hades moved closer. "So, William, what will it be?"

His mind reeled. He was free? The centuries of servitude were over? "What do you mean?"

Leaning against the counter, Hades crossed his arms. "You've got a choice now. Same as every other soul that comes to my realm. Go before the Judges, and move on to an eternal rest…somewhere. Given your history, I'm not sure they'll grant you admission to Elysium. It's up to them, of course, but you do have a lot of blood on your hands."

"What's the other choice?"

"You can become mortal again. Live the rest of the life you didn't have." He smiled. "I wonder how you would adapt to this world? Nine hundred years is a very long time. Your world lived by candlelight and traveled by horse. Hers is far more advanced." He pushed himself away and moved closer to William's face. "Don't make your choice based on feelings. You care for her. I know you do. But does she care for you?"

William. Yes, that's who he was now. If he stayed here, on the mortal plane, he could reclaim the honor he lost. And he'd made a promise to Amber. Whether or not he was Charon any more, he was still her Guardian. And that vow would remain his duty until she dismissed him.

"I am her Guardian, until she tells me otherwise. Her life is still in danger." He looked at her, surprised to see her face had changed. She could see Hades, hear what was being said. "Regardless of my feelings, I will respect hers. This is her world, her home. Anything else is secondary."

Hades sighed and moved away. "So be it done."

The unnatural silence abated as the god disappeared. Amber looked at him, her face full of wonder and curiosity. That conversation would have to wait, though.

"I get it. Didn't think you'd be the type of woman to ditch me like this, though." Heath said, anger driving the words.

"Heath, it's not what you're thinking. William and I—" A strange sound came from near her. Pulling a rectangular piece of metal out of her pocket, she touched it before putting it to her ear. "Hello?" Her head snapped up and she looked at William, alarm on her face, then over to

Heath. "Too late," she said, then put the device down on the counter.

"Why, Heath?"

His face tightened. "Why what?"

"Kate was looking through all the cards people left in her room. She found the one you sent. Told Sheriff Taylor that your handwriting was what was on the address of the package. Why'd you put the bomb outside the store?"

William stepped closer to Amber, ready to protect her.

"Damn it, Amber. You don't get it. You and I aren't meant for this town. We could spend winters in Australia… summers on a boat in the Rivera! You've got all the money we'd need to have a good life! But you couldn't see it. This town… The Cauldron… this house is the problem between us. I didn't think it would hurt Kate. I didn't even know what was in it. She told me to put it outside the store when I knew you'd be there. That she'd done the research and it'd force you to see reason and listen to me for a change."

"'She'?" Amber whispered. William saw her stiffen and the color drain from her face. She feared the answer.

"Her name was June. Said she was your best friend from Texas. That you'd been calling her, telling her how miserable you were up here during the winter."

"That wasn't a friend, Heath. That was my mother." Her voice rose. "How long?" she demanded. "Tell me how long you've been in contact with her!"

"Near as we can tell, the communication started within a month of you finishing the legal requirements for your inheritance." A man, wearing a uniform and a weapon of some kind on his hip, walked into the room. Two other men, one in a suit the other in a similar uniform, stood behind him.

"Get him out of my house please, Sheriff." Amber said through clenched teeth. She looked at the man in the suit. "Larry, can you stay?" She glanced over at William, "We need to talk, the three of us."

Heath stood. The third man put restraints of some kind around his wrists. "I did this for us, Amber. I didn't know it would hurt Kate."

She shook her head slowly. "No, Heath. You did this for yourself, to get what you wanted out of life. This wasn't about me at all. All you or my mom wanted was the money."

Watching the officers lead Heath away, William was struck by how different things were in the world now. He had so much to learn if he was going to stay here and survive. Which reminded him what he was going to ask her when he came downstairs.

"Guardian, this may be a bad time, but—"

She laughed. "My name's Amber. You need to use that over Guardian." Her tone softened and she relaxed after hearing a door close. Picking up the metal device, she tapped it a few times. She looked at the man in the suit. "Helps to actually use the security system," she said dryly. She took a deep breath. "Larry, I'd like you to meet William Jordan. At least, that's who he was over nine hundred years ago. Until last night, I knew him as Charon. It seems Hades has decided his punishment is at an end, and William's decided to give life another try. Can you help us get him legal status? Like you did when we changed my name?"

Larry nodded, "I'm sure we can work something out. It sounds like I've got a story to hear. Do you want to wait to tell it?"

William took a breath, "No. I'd like to start learning and living again. Guard … Amber ... I noticed you had an extensive library upstairs. Would you object if I started there?"

"No, that's fine. Probably a good place to begin. After Larry's done with us." She handed him a plate. "Here, eat something. I've got to unpack from the trip."

"So, William," Larry gestured to the dining area. "I need some details of your old life before I can establish a new one for you. Shall we get acquainted?"

Chapter Nineteen
Full Moon

Amber blew out the final candle surrounding her sacred space. After all that'd happened over the last month, she'd needed this. Especially tonight.

She and William discussed their relationship. They would always be connected. There was no denying that. And she did care for him. But what she needed right now wasn't a romance. It was space to grow and live life on her terms.

He'd told her how he felt. But that he understood why she wanted the space. His exact words told her so much. "I'd rather learn about this world, and see if you can love me, than ever force you to do so."

She was good with that.

They'd settled on being roommates. He took up residence in one of the spare bedrooms, devoting himself into catching up on centuries of history and learning about this new world he now lived in. Larry'd been able to establish his identity in the courts, similar to how he'd redone hers. It'd taken longer, but it was legal. Short of someone being entirely too nosy, no one should bother him. As long as he paid taxes, that is. For now, she'd pay the bills. Down the road, though, he wanted to go to school. Learn something that, as he put it, would make him feel like what he did made a difference.

Straightening, she doublechecked the candles before descending the staircase to her rooms. Maybe later on, when they both knew more of who they each really were, things would change.

The clock in her room read 11:55 pm. It was almost time.

Walking down the hall, she passed William's room. Through the open door, she saw him hunched over his desk. A book in front of him, notepad and pencil next to it. He took notes to ask her about later, usually over breakfast. Smiling, she kept walking.

Turning into the living room at the bottom of the staircase, she headed to the fireplace. Moving aside the brick, she pulled out the leather pouch. The mist was beginning to form out on the river.

She scratched Minerva's ears and headed to the back door. It was time for the Guardian to meet Charon again.

About the Author

Born in the late 60's, KateMarie has lived most of her life in the Pacific NW. While she's always been creative, she didn't turn towards writing until 2008. She found a love for the craft. With the encouragement of her husband and two children, she started submitting her work to publishers. When she's not taking care of her family, KateMarie enjoys attending events for the Society for Creative Anachronism. The SCA has allowed her to combine both a creative nature and love of history. She currently resides with her family and three cats in what she likes to refer to as "Seattle Suburbia".

You can find KateMarie at the following sites:

Twitter: @DaughterHauk
FaceBook: http://www.facebook.com/pages/KateMarie-Collins/217255151699492
Her blog: http://www.katemariecollins.wordpress.com
Via email: katemariecollins@gmail.com

Other Solstice Publishing Titles by KateMarie Collins

Guarding Charon

Arine's Sanctuary

Mark of the Successor
Consort of the Successor

Daughter of Hauk
Son of Corse
Wielder of Tiren
The Raven Chronicles

Fin's Magic
Alaric's Bow
Emile's Blade
Amari: Three Tales of Love and Triumph

Challenges Met
A Stab at the Dark
Looking at the Light
Kick the Can
The Rose Box
Permafrost
Siaira

CPSIA information can be obtained
at www.ICGtesting.com
Printed in the USA
FSHW020505260619
59446FS